Bottoms Up

Slocum jerked Horace up in his face so he could smell the whiskey breath on him. "Where's Bridges keep his money?"

"I don't know."

"You better get to recalling where it's at, or I'm pouring kerosene all over your privates and setting them on fire."

"You son of a bitch, you wouldn't do that to me."

"She would, if I don't."

"Oh, hell, I know who you are—you're Slocum. And that's the whore from—"

Slocum bashed him over the forehead with the barrel of his handgun and shoved him inside the barn's dark interior.

"Say one bad thing about this lady, and I'm sticking this gun up your ass and blowing your brains out the top of your head . . ."

DON'T MISS THESE
ALL-ACTION WESTERN SERIES
FROM THE BERKLEY PUBLISHING GROUP

THE GUNSMITH by J. R. Roberts
Clint Adams was a legend among lawmen, outlaws, and ladies. They called him . . . the Gunsmith.

LONGARM by Tabor Evans
The popular long-running series about Deputy U.S. Marshal Custis Long—his life, his loves, his fight for justice.

SLOCUM by Jake Logan
Today's longest-running action Western. John Slocum rides a deadly trail of hot blood and cold steel.

BUSHWHACKERS by B. J. Lanagan
An action-packed series by the creators of Longarm! The rousing adventures of the most brutal gang of cutthroats ever assembled—Quantrill's Raiders.

DIAMONDBACK by Guy Brewer
Dex Yancey is Diamondback, a Southern gentleman turned con man when his brother cheats him out of the family fortune. Ladies love him. Gamblers hate him. But nobody pulls one over on Dex . . .

WILDGUN by Jack Hanson
The blazing adventures of mountain man Will Barlow—from the creators of Longarm!

TEXAS TRACKER by Tom Calhoun
J.T. Law: the most relentless—and dangerous—manhunter in all Texas. Where sheriffs and posses fail, he's the best man to bring in the most vicious outlaws—for a price.

JAKE LOGAN

SLOCUM
AND THE
TRAIL TO TASCOSA

JOVE BOOKS, NEW YORK

THE BERKLEY PUBLISHING GROUP
Published by the Penguin Group
Penguin Group (USA) Inc.
375 Hudson Street, New York, New York 10014, USA
Penguin Group (Canada), 90 Eglinton Avenue East, Suite 700, Toronto, Ontario M4P 2Y3, Canada
(a division of Pearson Penguin Canada Inc.)
Penguin Books Ltd., 80 Strand, London WC2R 0RL, England
Penguin Group Ireland, 25 St. Stephen's Green, Dublin 2, Ireland (a division of Penguin Books Ltd.)
Penguin Group (Australia), 250 Camberwell Road, Camberwell, Victoria 3124, Australia
(a division of Pearson Australia Group Pty. Ltd.)
Penguin Books India Pvt. Ltd., 11 Community Centre, Panchsheel Park, New Delhi—110 017, India
Penguin Group (NZ), 67 Apollo Drive, Rosedale, North Shore 0632, New Zealand
(a division of Pearson New Zealand Ltd.)
Penguin Books (South Africa) (Pty.) Ltd., 24 Sturdee Avenue, Rosebank, Johannesburg 2196,
South Africa

Penguin Books Ltd., Registered Offices: 80 Strand, London WC2R 0RL, England

This is a work of fiction. Names, characters, places, and incidents either are the product of the author's imagination or are used fictitiously, and any resemblance to actual persons, living or dead, business establishments, events, or locales is entirely coincidental.

SLOCUM AND THE TRAIL TO TASCOSA

A Jove Book / published by arrangement with the author

PRINTING HISTORY
Jove edition / January 2011

Copyright © 2011 by Penguin Group (USA) Inc.
Cover illustration by Sergio Giovine.

ISBN: 978-0-515-14882-4

JOVE®
Jove Books are published by The Berkley Publishing Group,
a division of Penguin Group (USA) Inc.
375 Hudson Street, New York, New York 10014.
JOVE® is a registered trademark of Penguin Group (USA) Inc.
The "J" design is a trademark of Penguin Group (USA) Inc.

PRINTED IN THE UNITED STATES OF AMERICA

10 9 8 7 6 5 4 3 2 1

1

If there was anything different from Slocum's last time in North Platte, Nebraska, when he rode into town that early fall day, it was all the people. Thousands, it looked like to him, and a hundred more boomtown tents housed stores, saloons, whorehouses and dry goods. Farm implement dealers were there with spanking nice wagons neatly stacked on top of one another. New steel turning plows, harrows, drills, rakes and hay-mowing machines were all displayed—everything some foreign-talking honyocker needed to homestead, and down at the depot they were getting off the passenger trains like ants.

Plenty of Texas cowboys who'd driven herds of cattle up to stock the new ranges loafed around the town, looked for work and tried to decide if they should go back home before they got frozen in up there. Blue-winged teal were already gathering to fly south.

Slocum dismounted at Wilson's Wagon Yard, boarded his dun horse, Buck, for fifteen cents a day and strode back through the crowed boardwalk to the Red Lion Saloon. Inside the smoky interior, he made his way across the noisy, packed room to the bar and ordered a large beer. His plan was to wash down some road dust and see if the bartender on duty knew where he could find Charley Farley. The letter in the many times forwarded envelope in his inside vest pocket said his old trail-driving buddy would be easy to find.

"Hey, what do you need?" the weary-looking barkeep called to Slocum through the small window of open space between the backs of some horsy-smelling teamsters at the bar who were busy talking and hoisting their glasses.

"A tall beer and some information."

"I'll get the beer first," the mustached man said. "It'll be ten cents."

The price for a mug was the same anyway. Many times boomtowns jacked their prices up, claiming it was hard to get their supplies there.

Slocum put the dime on the bar and the man nodded, taking it to the till. It must be harder to collect bar bills in these crowded places. Cash on the line, he'd called it. Slocum looked around. There were several women working the crowd. Most of them were tough-looking women—but hell, a horny guy had no prejudice.

"Here's your beer, mister. What else?"

"Charley Farley. You know him?" Slocum asked over the noise of the crowd and an out-of-tune piano plinking away in the background.

The man acknowledged that he knew him. "But he's dead."

"How did that happen?"

"Shot, I guess. They have shootings all the time. . . . I've got to go. Ask the law."

"Sure. Thanks." The man was gone.

The sourness of the beer filled Slocum's mouth. It was cold, and he let it flush out his dusty throat going down. He held the mug up to the hazy light and watched the foam slide down the sides into the remains. *Here's to you, Farley. Sorry I'm too late for the final arrangements.*

He took another big swig of his beer. He'd better see about Charley's next of kin. Charley must have had some. The law in town would have that information. Slocum might even know some of the men with badges from three years before when he was up here last.

"Hey, big boy." A five-foot-three gal in a red fluffy dress began to adjust the sides of Slocum's wool vest and blocked his way. "I know you."

"Inform me. From where?" he said, looking down at her exposed divided cleavage.

She swept the light-colored hair back from her face and beamed up at him. "I'm Leta. Leta Couzki."

Leta Couzki? He couldn't recall any Leta. "Maybe you've got me mixed up with someone else?"

She clapped him on the arm and whispered, "Slocum, I'll never forget you, darling."

"Well, put that way, I guess you do know me." Then he laughed.

"Let's find a place we can talk." She motioned to the rear of the saloon.

"Sure," he said, then finished off his beer. He reached between the two clumps of back-to-back teamsters and set the glass on the bar.

"Catch me later," the bartender said over them. "I remember something about your man—the guy you mentioned."

"I will." He turned back to Leta. "You ate?"

She shook her head. "I could use a meal. You buying?"

"Sure. Is business that slow here?"

"Not really." She wrinkled her nose at him. "I'm too choosy. Come on, follow me."

She elbowed a path toward the swinging doors, cutting into the masses of close-packed customers. He grinned as she literally shoved men aside to make a passageway. A man would have drawn a fight if he'd done it like that, but the customers looked around at her, grinned real big and let them through.

Outside, she made another track through the people crammed on the boardwalk between the hitched horses at the rack and the walkway to finally emerge out in the street, looking both ways. "Wade's Diner. Best food in the entire area, and they're clean too. Come on, now's our chance."

The café she found for him was slack on business. In midafternoon business always fell off between lunch and supper. At an empty booth in the back, she scooted in midway and then had him sit across from her.

The waiter came over. Taking charge, she ordered coffee and a special plate lunch for both of them. After a check with Slocum to be certain it was all right with him, she sent the waiter off.

"What's your business in North Platte?" she asked, raising her leg up and hugging her skirt-clad knee above the tabletop.

"An old friend, Charley Farley, who they tell me is dead, asked me to come up here and help him."

"What did he need, for heaven's sake?"

"My help," he said.

"Everyone needs your help. What was he doing?"

"Trying to run cattle, I imagine."

She looked at the tin squares on the ceiling for help. "He needed a cowboy?"

"No, his trouble was with a large rancher."

"The Barr Ranch, huh?" She dropped her knee down and oversaw the waiter putting their steaming coffee cups on the table.

With the waiter gone again, she turned back to Slocum. "That bunch causes lots of trouble around here. What did he want you to do about it?"

"Help him, I guess, fight them."

"Well, you say he's dead. I didn't know him."

"Tell me, what are you doing working in a saloon?"

"I plan to open a place of my own here in town. So I've been finding me some investors. I don't work the teamsters and cowboys, dear, and I pay the owner twenty-five percent of what I earn. So he doesn't mind."

"How is that going? Finding investors."

"Damn good. This was my last day working over there." She smiled big at him. "Work starts on my house as soon as the lumber is delivered here by the railroad."

"Sounds good."

She pointed her finger at him. "You're the frosting on the cake. You and I are going to have a party tonight to celebrate. All right?"

The waiter appeared and set plates heaped high with sliced beef, mashed potatoes, flour gravy and green beans before them. "Anything else?"

After looking the setup over, she nodded her head. "Oh, bring us some bread and butter."

"Coming right up."

Looking a little put out with the man's interference, she exhaled out of her pert nose and then she made a displeased face after him. "Back to our party out at my tent. We'll get a couple of bottles of champagne and let the night flow. How will that be, darling?"

"I guess my business appointments can wait." The first forkful of food drew the saliva in his mouth. This was a good place to eat.

She laughed, and with her utensil in hand, she looked over the items on her plate. "Eat well. I have big plans for you tonight. What were yours?"

"Get a shave and a bath and clean up."

"Good idea. Do those things. I'll make you a map to my tent."

Slocum paused his eating. "Give me a couple of hours and I'll join you."

"Oh, that would be wonderful. You sure won't regret it."

After the meal, she stood on her toes and kissed him in the café doorway. "In two hours?"

"I've got your map. I'll be there."

They parted company, and Slocum decided to make a quick trip back to the Red Lion Saloon to ask the bartender what else he'd remembered about Charley. It turned out that the bartender remembered Charley mentioning that he had a wife—now his widow.

Next, Slocum went to the place with a painted sign that read BATHS. The Orientals who ran the bathhouse were very polite, and a small woman in wooden-soled shoes showed him to his tub. "They bring you water. Here you soap. I put towel on this chair."

The room smelled musty like old gray water. A small window over Slocum's head was open, and the town's street noises drifted in. The woman left, and he began to undress. Soon two girls with steaming buckets came in and poured the contents into his tub. They bowed and left.

He shed the towel from around his waist and eased himself into the hot water. No telling what he'd do next—besides go to Leta's party. Why had Farley been shot? Had the big rancher shot his friend or hired the one who shot him? These were things he needed to know in order to avenge his friend's death.

Settled in the tub, he closed his eyes and let the vapors go up his nose. This was heaven. At last he'd found it. The heat felt wonderful on his stiff back muscles. Nebraska had never been this good to him before.

He'd have to see about Farley later.

Udall Barr sat at his rolltop desk in the corner of the large living room and closed the ranch's ledger book. A five-foot-nine man in his thirties, he listened to the springs in his swivel chair protest as he leaned back and tented his fingers together like a spider on a mirror. Erma, the farm girl who'd begun working at the Barr Ranch a couple of months ago, walked in carrying coffee, and it reminded Barr of the first time he'd had sex with Erma.

That day nearly two months ago, he'd been sitting in his desk chair just as he was today, but his thoughts hadn't been on the expenses he'd recorded in his ledger—it was fixed on having sex. How long since he'd had any? The last time must have been two, three days before. He'd looked up at the underside of the cedar shingle roof. His log house was snug. It had to be for this cold climate, but he wanted a majestic two-story mansion like them rich folks in Dallas and Fort Worth lived in.

Leaning back, he dreamed of having all that, with a young wife to wait on him.

"Mr. Barr?" It was Erma, the newly hired farm girl, coming across the room. His housekeeper, Mozelle, had hired Erma to help her. A little on the chubby side for his taste, nonetheless she was all he had besides his hand to relieve his horniness that afternoon.

He twisted the chair around to face her. "Yes, Erma?"

"Did you want some coffee or anything?"

"No, Erma. Come over here."

Hesitant and wringing her hands in a rag, she chewed on her lower lip. "Is something wrong, Mr. Barr?"

He waved her closer. "Nothing is wrong. You know I really like you?"

She shook her head, gazing at the floor. "I really like working here, Mr. Barr."

He patted his leg. "Come sit on my lap."

"Oh, I could never do that."

"You like working here, don't you?" He gave her a serious frown to send her the signal that he was not pleased with her refusal.

"Yes, sir."

"Then come sit on my lap."

"I sure am embarrassed doing this." She took a place on his knee and chewed harder on her lower lip.

He bounced her a little on his leg, then he cupped her face in his hands, pulled her over and kissed her on the mouth. It was like smooching with a cold fish. Her eyes flew open in shock.

"Oh." At last she gasped for air. When she tried to get up, he forced her to remain seated on his lap.

"We're going to have a good time this afternoon. Do you understand?"

"What—what are we going to do?"

"Oh, you'll like it, my dear. Stay still now."

"But—but—"

"Close your eyes."

"What are you going to—?"

He felt her firm breast beneath the dress material and smiled. Her hand clasped his to restrain his actions.

"Now, Erma, you need this job here, don't you?"

"Oh, I do, sir."

He tapped her nose with his index finger. "Your job depends on how you act toward me this afternoon. Do you understand?"

She swallowed hard. "I-I do."

"Unbutton your dress."

She hesitated, then her fingers fumbled with the buttons. He pushed the dress off her shoulders, and he could feel her shaking, seated there on his leg.

"Now take off your chemise."

Aghast, she looked at him in shock. "But I'll be naked." He nodded.

She closed her eyes and took her chemise off over her head. Gently he fondled her rock-hard tits; she held her breath the entire time. Her nipples began to harden. When she started to speak in protest, his finger on her mouth silenced her. He untied the string at her waist that held up her underwear.

"Stand up and let's see what we have here."

Hugging her pear-shaped breasts, she stepped out of the

underwear, which had fallen around her ankles, and the dress fell to the floor. Bare assed, she didn't look half bad; her belly made a curve outward, but not as bad as Barr had imagined.

He led her over to the couch. "Lie down on the Indian rug."

With his toe he pushed off his boots, watching her as she sat down on the rug, lifting her brown hair from her neck. His shirt came off and his pants followed, then he slid his underwear down and his great erection stood at attention.

"Lie on your back," he said and wondered if she would obey him.

She did, but on her back she glanced at his hard-on for the first time and screamed. Before she could back out on him, he was already on his knees and had spread her legs apart, ready to nose his stiff dick inside her. His first effort at entry drew a sharp cry of pain from her, but in minutes she was moaning in pleasure's arms while he pumped into her slow and steady. Thoroughly enjoying himself, he plunged away, gripping her ass and lifting her legs up higher so he could go deeper. Soon their pubic bones were grinding the coarse hair between them.

Then she cried out and flat fainted. Still with the stone ache plaguing his left nut, he braced himself over her. "Wake up, you silly girl."

"Oh," she moaned, barely opening her eyelids, and he restarted his plunger. Closing his own eyes, he went faster and harder, straining against her until at last his rocket went off and they collapsed in a pile.

Groggy and spent, he climbed up on his knees and looked down at her shielding her nakedness. "Tonight you will sleep in my bed with me."

"Yes," she said in surrender. "May I dress now?"

"Don't wear any underwear from now on." He grinned at her. "I might want your butt sometime in a hurry. Understand?"

"Yes."

Dumb bitch. She'd entertain him for a while. When he got tired of her ass, he'd ship her off.

Nearly two months later, Barr was still enjoying the benefits of a live-in mistress. As directed, Erma never wore underwear anymore, and she knew that when she brought him coffee when he was idle at his desk, they'd most likely end up on the rug with the both of them naked. Today was no exception.

When he was finished with her, he dressed and went out into the yard. His foreman, Selman Doss, had ridden in and was unsaddling his bay horse at the saddle shed. Barr walked down there in the bright midday sun to talk with his man.

"We got any problems?" Barr leaned back against the corral rails and hooked his right boot heel on a lower one.

Doss yawned. "That CT bunch is crowding us some. I seen maybe thirty pairs on this side of Welch Creek."

"Push them back west. They don't stay off, we'll go find Thomas and tell him either he keeps them home or we send them home, and he won't like that."

"He's kinda tough."

"Shit, all them Texans are tough. But they can't stop a .45 bullet right between their eyes." Barr slapped the top rail of the corral to make his point.

"You're right, boss, you're right."

Barr looked at the windswept hills to the north. "We're going to need to bring more pressure on that Farley woman to get the hell off that claim of hers and to sell us her cows."

"She's damn hardheaded."

"I been thinking how to get rid of her. Why don't you hire four guys to go over there wearing masks and have all of them rape her ass raw."

"I could do that. There's some toughs drifting into the country. I can hire them, no questions asked. What're you willing to pay 'em?"

"Forty bucks a man. But I want her ass so sore that she gets off that place."

Doss nodded. "I'll get 'em."

"Be damn sure it don't point a finger at us. And I don't want them killing no one."

"I'll watch that they don't."

"Just you be sure to do that." Barr stalked off for the house. Sometimes he wished he had a tougher foreman; Doss could be too slow at times to suit him.

He downed two half glasses of whiskey while standing at the polished cabinet in the living room, and then he paced the floor. What was wrong? Why was he so damn nervous? Things were going good. He was building a great grass empire. And he had a live-in pet—Erma, the onetime virgin.

What had him so upset? He wasn't certain, but come nightfall he'd have Erma in his bed and he'd work her ass over good again. The notion gave him half an erection simply thinking about it.

He set the glass down and refilled it to halfway, then popped the cork back in the bottle. That was enough. That was plenty.

2

Slocum found Leta's tent, bringing two bottles of champagne in his saddlebags, some prairie flowers he'd picked, along with two fresh-baked loaves of French bread and a pound of butter. When he rode in closer to her tent, she stepped into the opening, hands on her hips, wearing some lacy gown he could see through.

"Where did you get the flowers?" She squinted from the front flap, using the side of her hand as a shield against the bleeding sun going down.

He stepped off Buck and she ran over, more impressed with the damned flowers than the expensive French champagne he'd bought. He slipped the saddle and bridle off his horse and stood it on the saddle horn. Buck wouldn't go anywhere. Then they walked back to the tent with her carrying the flowers, bread and butter while he brought the two long-stem crystal glasses wrapped in Turkish towels, plus the bottles of bubbly, one under each arm.

"This where you're going to build?" He looked over the countryside.

"Naw. I'm building it on Main Street in town. This was

isolated and a good place to entertain my investors. No nosy neighbors out here, so if our Roman lovemaking spills out of the tent tonight, nobody will notice us." She threw back her head and laughed. "Where have you been since I saw you in Abilene—or was that Hayes?"

"You name it, I've been there, from Canada to deep in Mexico."

"Here, let me put these flowers in a jar with water. Gaw-damn you! Bringing me flowers—I could cry." She kept her back to him.

"Why?"

"'Cause that's neat and reminds me of the first boy I ever kissed. Billy Shanks, a big, lanky farm boy, brought me a mess of fresh flowers that evening he came courting. Oh, I bawled about that too. I was a tomboy, about eighteen or maybe past. A boy never brought me nothing before that, they always expected me to pitch in all their baseball games 'cause I was the best striker-out they had. But none of them ever acted sweet on me until Shanks came by with them flowers. I didn't know what to expect, so I put the flowers up and told the folks I'd be back.

"We walked down to the crick where there was a swim-ming hole. It was a hot night. Billy hemmed and hawed until he finally got out that we ought to go swimming, buck naked. I'd never been swimming with them boys. Oh, I'd been skinny-dipping with my cousin Isabel at night some-times, but never naked with any boy.

"We started daring each other and double daring the other to get undressed and be the first in the crick. By damn, no boy was going to beat me. I wore overalls and he did too, but his hung up on him and he had to sit down to get them off his ankles. Undressed, I charged out in the water in a big splash and swam to the far side. He dove in and we met in the middle of the crick.

"I never knew how it happened, but I caught hold of his long, limber dick underwater. Felt dumb holding it, but he bent over and kissed me for doing it, I guess. Next thing I knew, he was packing me out of there, dripping wet, and I lost my virginity on the grassy bank that night. No big deal, he was gentle with me, but we did it four times that night. I was pretty heady over enjoying it so much when I snuck back in the house after midnight."

"You and him get serious?"

"Yeah, for a while." She sliced the bread and he worked on uncorking the first bottle of champagne. "But, you know, there ain't much for a dumb boy and a dumb girl in Missouri to do but get married, have a baby every year and fuck at night when the kids are finally asleep. I wanted more than that for my life." Her hand extended, she gave him a bite off the end of the buttered slice.

"Mmm, that's good." Slocum chewed, then gripped the bottle and pulled until the cork flew out. He quickly poured the bubbly into a glass for her and then some into his own.

"I still can't get over you bringing me flowers."

"Obviously, it impressed you." He raised this glass to hers. "Here's to a real party."

Sometime later during the night, in all their nakedness and lovemaking on a narrow cot—wide enough for one, deep enough for two—they finished off a healthy coupled event and fell asleep in each other's arms. When Slocum awoke in the predawn, he stepped outside and emptied his bladder in the cool wind sweeping over his bare skin. Winter wasn't far away. Looking up at the bright stars, he could almost smell it.

Maybe he'd go into town that morning and find Charley's widow, if he wasn't too distracted. Slocum needed to talk to the law too. Was Charley's shooting self-defense or murder? He had lots of questions with no answers. Buck raised his head up from grazing and nickered at him. Yeah, he saw him. Good, he hadn't run off anyway.

"Bust some short wood. I'll make us some breakfast." Leta stood in the open flap wrapped in a blanket.

"Ugh," he said like an Indian.

Her laughter carried as she went back inside to dress. He stood in the open flap and watched her put the dress on over her head and wiggle it down over her shapely body in the flickering candlelight. He put on his pants and his shirt, then he strapped on the gun belt, and the next-to-last item was the vest. Setting his Stetson on his head, he ducked and went outside.

In a short time, he had lots of stove wood chopped into usable pieces.

Leta came by and took an armload. "You can stick around. You're good help."

Under a canvas fly, she had a cookstove with a tin tent patch to let the stovepipe stick up from her range. She was busy making bread in a big wash pan on the dry sink when he brought in some more wood.

"Dump that ground coffee from the grinder's drawer in the pot. The water's boiling," she said over her shoulder.

"I can do that."

"You know, you're handy as a shirt pocket."

"I guess," he said absently, his mind on other matters.

It was kind of serious about Charley Farley being dead. . . . He and Charley had ramrodded some herds to Kansas for the same outfit. Good man, tough as rawhide and friendly as any guy living, unless you double-crossed him or made him mad. He and Charley'd cleaned out a saloon in Wichita that had been skinning their drovers out of their pay—and then they got those boys half their lost *dinero* back for them. It was kind of serious that Charley went and got himself killed. That notion niggled at him more and more by the hour. There had to be answers to it all. He simply needed to find them.

Barr never woke up in a good mood, and this morning was no exception. Even sleeping with Erma as he had for the last two months had not changed his bear-emerging-from-hibernation disposition. Maybe the fact that when he threw his hand over to locate her ass in the bed and discovered nothing was there added to his sour mood. He could hear Erma and his housekeeper whispering in the kitchen and the muffled sounds of pots and pans being scraped across the range top. Barefoot, he pulled on his pants and, standing straddle legged, he put on his shirt, tucked the tail in, drew his britches up and buttoned the fly, then slipped the suspenders over his shoulders. Seated on the complaining bed, he shook out his socks, put them in place and then pulled on his high-top boots.

He could hear his housekeeper ringing the triangle. His crew would be down in a short while to eat breakfast. Thinking about all he needed to do that day, he strapped on his gun belt.

What would produce fear in the bastards crowding his range? His plans for the multiple rape of that Farley woman would send her ass packing. But there were lots more who needed to be moved out, and quickly. And all them other homesteaders moving in—this was cattle range, not farmland.

"Here's your eggs, ham and biscuits," his housekeeper, Mozelle, announced, handing him the platter when he came into the room. He took his place at the head of the long table and looked over the sleepy-eyed ranch crew busy filling their faces.

"You boys ready to give me a full day's work?"

"Yes, sir, Mr. Barr," came the chorus.

Scrambled eggs poised on his fork, he looked them over. "See that you do." Then he fed his mouth and ignored them.

Two hours later, Barr used his field glasses to search for the source of the campfire smoke he could smell. They were camped on his land. If he let them stay there very long, more settlers would pour into this bottom along Hungry Boy Creek. He could see a man standing talking to a bonneted woman bent over a cooking fire stirring a kettle and some kids going about other camp chores. With care he slipped back to his blood bay horse and eased the Remington sniper rifle out of the scabbard. Like an Injun he stole his way back to the point, set up the two sticks he used for a rest and found the man in the telescopic sight. Rifle loaded, he cocked the set trigger, and then the impact of the heavy caliber's stock's butt slammed into Barr's shoulder.

Wind swiftly carried the gun smoke away, and in the distance he heard the woman wailing. One less honyocker in Nebraska that morning anyway. Barr mounted up and slipped away, leaving so few tracks that even an Injun would have found him hard to track down. At last, with the rifle securely wrapped in its waxed canvas sheath and hidden back under the line shack's floor, he rode on into town.

North Platte bustled with people—if he had his way he'd have shoved every one of them back on trains and shipped them back East. He'd maybe even have used cattle cars for those who didn't fit on the passenger trains, and he'd have kept patrols set up to hold them all east of Omaha.

"Barr, you must have been busy. I ain't seed your ass in over half a week," the livery swamper said, taking his horse's reins.

"And it ain't none of your gawdamn business what I do." He reached out, caught the old man's suspenders in his fists and jerked him in up in his face. "What I do is my own affair and not none of yours, savvy?"

"I savvy plenty good. But some old man of your outfit has made the mayor of North Platte mad as hell, they tell me."

"Sumbitch. What did he do?"

"Traded off the mayor's favorite Chinese whore for a sheep."

"What in the hell are you talking about?" Barr let the man go and frowned at him.

"Aw, hell, ain't you got any sense of humor in ya?"

"No. And I don't need none." He stomped off down Main Street, which was choked with newcomers and rigs. Why, it would take a thousand rounds of ammo to even make a dent in all these sonsabitches.

3

Slocum found the sheriff's office bustling with the drunks and rabble-rousers arrested the night before, who were going one by one before a justice of the peace to be fined or sentenced. They posed as a sorry, hungover lot.

"Keep in that line," a burly deputy ordered, beating a club in his palm.

"Who's the sheriff these days?" Slocum asked the man.

"Huey Garner. He's in his office."

"Thanks." Good, he knew the chief lawman. Slocum strode over to the desk officer.

"Can I help you?" The young man in a white shirt and tie behind the desk barely looked up from his paperwork.

"Tell Sheriff Garner that Slocum is here to see him."

The desk man stood up. "I'll see what he says."

A familiar, mustached lawman in a suit coat soon came to the office doorway and looked at Slocum. "What brings you back to Nebraska, Slocum? Come in here."

"Good times, I guess." Slocum looked over Garner's office, which was lined with racks of long guns. "Man, this place is overrun with people."

"The government took all the land south of the Dakota border away from the Sioux and opened it up." Garner pointed to the large map on the wall. "It's been a madhouse ever since. What brings you here?"

"Charley Farley. I understand that he was recently shot."

"In the back, of course, with a high-powered rifle. His buckboard came home without him. His wife and three hands went to look for him. They found where he fell off the buckboard, but we never found where the shooter had been waiting for him."

"No suspects?"

"Maybe a million or more. I sent my best men out there, and they found nothing. But that isn't the first case of these long-range killings in this district. Counting Farley, it makes five in the past nine months. Doc says it was a high-powered rifle and an accurate shooter. Have a chair."

Slocum took the one he offered. "Who were the others that got shot?"

"A real estate man named Johnson, a drifter cowboy, a surveyor, a schoolteacher. Does that make any sense?"

"Maybe they simply want to scare folks away?"

"I thought about that too. This killer is a dead shot. Each victim either had a head wound or was chest shot."

"The schoolteacher—I wonder why that one."

"He was putting up the American flag, and the kids were inside the building. *Bang!* They heard the shot, and he was on the ground. They rushed to the doorway, then scampered back inside—afraid they'd be next. Finally one of the older boys went out to check on the teacher. He came back and told the rest of them that Mr. Taylor was dead. They ain't found a new teacher yet."

"Sounds to me like you've got a real killer, one with a grudge against somebody or something."

"You want a badge?" Garner offered.

"No, but I want to investigate Farley's death some more."

"I'd love for you to do that. I want that killer off my back too."

"Did Farley ever complain about being pressured by a large rancher?"

"Not formally, like swore out a warrant or anything. Him and Barr had words over some water rights. In court the judge gave the water rights to Farley. But that's not a real reason to kill a man—at least, I couldn't see accusing Barr of Farley's death when Barr had an alibi for that whole day and solid witnesses."

"I guess I need to meet this Barr. Farley referred to him in his letter."

"Barr's a Texan, in his thirties. Came up here with some money a few years ago and made some money on his cattle deals. He's a shrewd trader. I think he wants an empire in this grass. He's also an arrogant SOB, but I've never caught him stepping over the law."

"So you're stuck with him?"

"I guess. Andy, bring some coffee for me and Slocum," he said to his clerk outside the door.

"Black?" the man asked from the doorway.

"Fine," Slocum said. "Where can I start? I don't know Farley's wife."

"She's from Texas. I'm certain from her drawl. Minnie Farley—nice lady—was with her former husband, and they were bringing a herd up here, two years ago, I'd say. Somewhere on or near the Colorado line, her husband was killed in a horse wreck, and when she arrived in North Platte, Farley offered to help her. That struck up a wedding."

Slocum sat back in the chair and soon sipped the strong, hot coffee. "The West as we know it will soon be taken up by God-fearing folks."

"You know, with every dozen God-fearing families that come in here," Garner said, "at least one worthless lot arrives. Horse stealing is so bad north of here that folks can't keep stock. I don't have enough deputies to cover half this new land, and no money to pay them either."

"I saw your business from last night out in the hall."

Garner pursed his lips and shook his head. "That's only a small part of it."

The coffee tasted good and opened Slocum's mind, which had been numbed by his overactive night madness in bed with Leta. He could still recall the flavor of her mouth, even with his own filled with Garner's rich brew. Last night it had brought back a crystal clear memory of the last time he'd seen her, some time ago now.

After the round of refreshment, the lawman drew Slocum a map to Farley's place and Slocum thanked him, promising to be around if Garner needed him.

Garner walked him to the door to see him off. "I may need you. My chief deputy, Sam Welch, can answer any questions about the murder. He was out there."

"Sheriff! Sheriff!" Someone driving a buckboard with lathered horses was standing up, shouting for the sheriff as he fought the traffic to reach him.

"What is it?" Garner asked, sharing a puzzled look with Slocum, who also came into the street to see what was wrong.

"That damn sniper has shot another man this morning," the excited farmer shouted, indicating the body in the back of his buckboard.

The corpse in the back was a tall man in overalls. Under his black beard his face was snow-white, and his eyes were closed. The massive wound in his chest and the dark blood dried on the overall bib told Slocum a high-powered bullet had torn out part of his lungs.

"Everyone get back," the sheriff shouted. "All of you!"

A murmur ran through the crowd. Slocum heard it. It was nothing he hadn't been exposed to before under similar circumstances—*We need to hang the sumbitch who did this dastardly crime*.

"Who is he, Norman?" Garner asked.

"Name's Kennedy, Howard Kennedy. Got a wife and a mess of kids. They were going to settle near me on Hungry Boy Creek."

In disgust, Garner dropped his head, until at last he looked up. "I better go investigate. You want to ride along?" he asked Slocum.

"I guess. Don't know what I can do, but sure, I'll go."

"Take him to Dr. Schmidt, then have them get him ready for the funeral. What about his wife and family?"

"She's coming behind me. And got a boy of fifteen who's driving the whole family into town with their rig."

"Where did this happen?"

"At the Hatcher Spring."

"I'll get a few things and tell my staff, Slocum. Meet you at the livery in five minutes."

Slocum excused the lawman and led Buck up to the livery to wait for the sheriff. Lots of things happening—another man shot, and as odd a one as the list of past victims; this killer must have a hard-on against everybody in this land. Who in hell could it be?

A sunbeam shone on the swirling dust particles in the column of light coming through the bank's high window. Barr sat in the captain's chair across from Amos Toothacker, the president of the institution. Toothacker was a short man with a bushy gray beard who reminded Barr of a fat old groundhog perched on a rise. At times, Toothacker even held his hands like a rodent standing up did.

"Money is very short nationwide," Toothacker lamented. "Conditions on the stock market are bad right now. We may have to charge very high interest for any loans we can arrange for you. Things are serious these days."

"Every time I have a chance to make some real money, it's always the economy that screws me up."

"I know. I know what you mean. Volatile times. It's volatile times, my boy."

"When will you know about the money? Any stranded herds up here will be available for a quick sale when the first cold draft comes out of the Dakotas."

"I have wires out. Money is simply damn tight. I am working as hard as I can on the matter. This entire country is in a serious recession."

"I'll check back with you." Barr rose and put on his hat. Times like these he'd like to strangle that little weasel to death. He'd better go have a drink and find himself a piece of pussy. Maybe then he could forget Toothacker for a little while.

"I'm working on it. Working hard." The banker stood up and accompanied him to the door of his office.

Damn sure not hard enough.

4

Slocum and Sheriff Garner headed out of town across the Platte River bridge. The lawman rode a big black horse that looked stout. On the road, Garner exchanged casual pleasantries with the many people who knew him—it was part of a politician's job. There was lots of traffic, and many people camped alongside the road were hitching up after having breakfast to head north in search of land. Some families with as little as a handcart were on the road. How would they ever survive the coming winter? Slocum wondered.

They weren't his worry—but he'd be niggled all day thinking about their welfare in the future. It was too late in the year to start any garden. . . . Hell, he'd forget them—if he could.

"Like you said, things are changing," Garner said. "Only thing I ever recall on this road a few years ago were cattle and freighters headed for the army forts."

"And changing fast." Slocum nudged Buck to trot a little faster to keep up.

On the road, they met the family of the dead man, with the boy driving their loaded farm wagon. The red-faced

27

woman wearing a bonnet, who'd no doubt been crying, held a small youngster in her arms. Four other children surrounded the seat.

Garner introduced himself and dismounted.

They all climbed down, and Mrs. Kennedy, between her sobs, told of how she'd been cooking breakfast and her husband had bolted forward—hit hard in the chest. Then she heard the report of the rifle, and her husband had spilled on the ground.

"He never said a word." She sniffed in a rag. "Howard was dead like that. We have no enemies. We were merely moving through. . . . Why did they do that?"

"I don't know, ma'am. Did you see anyone?"

"No. I don't even know what direction the bullet came from."

"You saw no one?"

"Nothing. It came like a thunderbolt out of nowhere."

"Slocum and I are going to ride up there and look for clues. You were camped at those springs?"

"Yes, sir," the youth said. "I never saw a thing either. I was hitching the team at the time."

"There had to be someone at the trigger." Garner folded his arms over his chest and shook his head. "Which direction was your husband facing?"

"West," she said. "Why?"

"He was shot in the back?"

"Yes."

"Then the shooter was east of your camp."

"I don't know."

"Neither do I. Mrs. Kennedy, your husband's body will be at the Burns Funeral Home. They'll handle things. I'm sorry, but we need to ride up there and look for some clues."

"I understand." She herded her small children back, so they could leave.

"You're doing a nice job," Garner said to the young man.

"Thank you, sir. I'll take good care of them."

Slocum agreed and helped Mrs. Kennedy back up on the wagon seat, then handed up the children too small to climb up.

When they were mounted and on the road again, Garner looked back to check to be sure that he and Slocum were alone. "I get sick thinking how they'll exist without a man."

"You aren't the only one."

At the springs, though the camp was tramped up, they did find a place where Kennedy's dark blood stained the ground, and they took an aim at the coverage on the hillside. Enough cedars up there to cover a shooter, Slocum decided. He gave a head toss to Garner, mounted up and rode east. He dismounted and let Buck graze. Knowing the distance of most sniper rifles, he felt he was close to the spot.

Then he found some fresh bent grass and a heel print—only the back rim, but it was a sloping boot heel. Circling wide, he spotted the side of a sole indent in the ground. Slocum squatted down, and Garner joined him.

"Find something?"

"Someone in boots was up here earlier." Slocum rose and moved east, looking hard at the ground between the knee-high grass for more tracks. "Here's another heel print."

"Damn," Garner swore. "I've hired Indians couldn't have found them."

"We ain't found the boot wearer yet. He kept a horse in this area. It was shod too." Slocum pointed out the signs.

"Where did he go next?"

"I'd say east."

They followed the horse's tracks until they spotted the line shack.

"Whose place is that?" Slocum reined up his dun.

"I imagine Barr's. The shooter go there?"

"I guess we'll know in a short while."

Inside the shack, there was nothing disturbed that they could find.

"He didn't stay here long or eat anything," Slocum said, standing in the open doorway and looking across the rolling grassy hills. There had to be some reason for the shooter to stop over at this place, but it damn sure wasn't obvious to him at the moment.

"But he stopped here. Why?"

"I guess we'll have to ask him that when we find him."

Garner chuckled. "Well, any more prints that we can track?"

"I think he went to the road from here and on into North Platte."

"All we need is a face, huh?" Garner led the way down to the hitched horses.

Mounted up, they rode for town.

"I appreciate your tracking," Garner said when they reached the road again. "Not much chance we can find that pony by looking at all the shoes, is there?"

"It would have to be pretty unusual shoes." Slocum looked over his shoulder. Nothing back there. "I guess I'll go find Farley's widow in the morning." Either the hit man had a reason to go back to that shack or there was something there that drew him to this place. Maybe Slocum needed to make a better search of that shack? The next time, he'd look it over in less of a hurry.

"I'll buy you supper when we get back to town," Garner said.

"I never turn down a meal, especially a free one." They both laughed.

Barr had picked her out. She was some short slut working in the Lucky Horse who flirted around him like a bumblebee. Called herself Henny.

"Will you do it for two bits?" he asked, whispering in her hair, which stank of stale smoke.

"Hell, I've got to pay rent," she complained. "How about six bits?"

"Why, darling, you'll still have all evening to catch the dumb ones."

"Six bits."

"All right, but you better be hotter than a fox bitch in heat."

"I won't disappoint ya."

He looked around. "Where's your pen?"

"Across the alley."

"Lead the way."

He watched the crowd closely as they slid to the back. This wasn't going to be some quick fix and then him getting robbed. First, he wasn't drunk, and she knew it. Second, he didn't wear a gun for looks. It better not be no fiasco, or she'd end up in the Platte facedown. No one ever investigated the murders of whores; they were expendable.

In her small room, which smelled of women's piss, cheap perfume and sour sweat, he hung his gun belt on the chair rung. He watched her undress as he undid his pants. She wasn't that bad, kind of potbellied, and her breasts sagged. Soon undressed, she came over to him as he finished stepping out of his long johns.

"You got a big tool, mister." She nodded at his pecker.

"I bet it ain't too big for your hole."

"If I'd known it was that big, I'd of charged you more." She dropped on her ass on the bed when he shooed her that direction.

"Get on your back and spread them knees. This ain't going to be no dick dipping like you get by with from them dumb farm boys."

"What—what do you mean?"

"I know your kind. You let them stick their pecker in a little ways and then you drop your legs so they ain't hardly got their pecker inside. And they get their rocks off."

He kneeled on the bed and gathered her legs in the crooks of his arms. She cut off a cry. He hunched at her until at last he nosed his half-full erection into her gates. With a great effort, he finally drove his dick halfway home and took her breath away. Then he went to pounding her ass until he was hammering on the bottom with the head of his swollen rod.

Out of breath, she was tossing her head and moaning. He grinned to himself; it wasn't easy to get a slut like her wound up. Then he felt the tingling in his balls and he came hard.

"Whew," she said when he disengaged from her and let her legs drop. "That was something."

He found the money in his pants pocket and slapped it on the small dresser. "You ain't half bad, bitch. Next time, take a bath and I'll pay you a buck."

"Huh?" She scratched her frizzy hair.

Dressed at last, he buckled on his gun. She didn't get it. The dumb bitch didn't understand what he meant. Maybe he ought to drag her ass down and hold her underwater in the river awhile. It would take a real stiff brush to ever get even her ass clean. Hell, he didn't have time for that.

"Remember me. My name's Henny," she shouted after him.

But he never acknowledged her as he went on out.

Barr headed up the shadowy alley. It would be dark soon. His snitch, Hooker, would meet him at the back of the stables. Any news he needed to know, his man would have the information or would find it out.

He saw a match light and nodded to himself. Hooker was there, back in the deep shadows. Barr joined him.

"What's happened?" Barr looked all around.

"Some farmer got shot. The sniper got him, I heard."

"What else?"

"Some tough hand named Slocum rode up there with Garner."

"Who's he? Slocum."

"He helped Garner break up a horse rustling gang three years ago."

"He some kinda federal law?"

"Naw," Hooker said. "Just some guy drifting through that Garner knows."

"I'll have to look for him."

"Big guy. Tough too."

"But you don't know why he's here?"

They both went quiet as an old drunk stumbled past, muttering all the way, and never saw them. They waited till he was gone.

"Charley Farley sent for him."

"When?"

"Damned if I know. But it had to be before he got shot."

Barr shook his head. "What'll he do about it?"

Hooker shrugged. "I figure he's going to dig some."

Maybe he should stop the plan to gang-rape Farley's widow. No, she needed it—and what the hell could one man do anyway, even one who was a buddy of the damn sheriff? But he'd have to watch for him. "Slocum, huh?"

"That's the only name I caught."

He'd never heard of this guy before. Maybe one of his crew had heard of him. One thing he knew—he'd damn sure go to checking around about him.

"What about the farmer who got shot?"

"Kennedy. He got buried this afternoon."

"Good riddance. I'll see you in a few days." Barr paid him five dollars. Cheap for all the information he got off the old guy. Sumbitch knew everything that happened in North Platte, or found it out. He was worth all that Barr gave him.

Barr went between the two buildings and then inside the Texas Moon Saloon, where he bought two bottles of good whiskey. The barkeep wrapped each one in a Turkish towel and then tied them with string so they'd nest in his saddlebags. It'd be after midnight before he got back to the ranch. That was all right. He had jerky to chew on; he wouldn't starve. Besides, Erma's cunt would be waiting for him.

Riding across the toll bridge, he stood in the stirrups and reached inside his waistband to solve the itch in his privates. Drawing his hand out, he wrinkled his nose at the stink. Whew! That bitch Henny sure did need a bath.

5

Slocum left town long before dawn, headed for Minnie Farley's ranch headquarters. Buck acted spirited in the cool morning air. His rest and the grain he'd been fed had restored his liveliness. Earlier he'd come close to bucking when Slocum swung his leg over him in the street outside the stables.

The evening before, Leta had been involved with some of her investors, so Slocum had spent the night in a livery bunk. Rising early, Slocum had caught a fast breakfast before mounting Buck and swinging north.

Midmorning, he dropped off the rise and could see the low-walled ranch house, corrals and outbuildings. From Garner's map, he knew it was Farley's place, all right—but there was no wood smoke coming out of the chimney. Something was badly wrong. He drew his .44 Colt out of the holster and checked to be certain it was ready. Then he cut across the slope to make sure he wasn't riding into a trap. From there he could see in the distance that the front door stood wide open. Not a dog barked. Only a Jersey cow bawled like someone had forgotten to milk her.

He edged the dun downhill. Some horses in the corral whinnied at Buck, who answered them softly. The first stock dog he spotted had been shot several times and was lying in the dirt near the front door. There were lots of fresh tracks from horses churning up the yard. He dropped heavily out of the saddle. The skin on the back of his neck itched as he looked all around. Overnight something terrible had happened at this place.

His .44 in his fist, Slocum edged to the doorway and tried to adjust his eyes to the room's darkness. A naked woman was tied to the four corners of the bed with torn sheets.

He holstered the six-gun and stepped closer. There was no doubt in his mind; she had been repeatedly raped and then left bound there by her attackers. Was she even alive? He felt for her pulse in her closest wrist. There was some throbbing.

From his belt, he swept out a knife and cut her hands and feet loose, moving around her, slicing the bindings and then holstering the knife.

Her eyelids fluttered open. "Who—who are you?" She sat up and quick-like reached for a sheet to cover herself.

"I'm not looking at you. Who did this?" He covered her with another flannel sheet and she hugged it, coughing deep. Feeling deep sympathy for her, he clapped her arms to reassure her.

"Where are your ranch hands?"

"Oh, my God, they may have killed them all—" She tried to scoot off the bed, but he caught her.

"Easy. I'll go find them. You rest. I'll be right back."

"Oh—if they're dead—"

"Stay right there," he said, using both hands to force her to remain on the bed, and she fell back limply.

Satisfied that she was too weak to argue with him, he backed out and then hurried out the door to get a breath of fresh air. His lungs needed it. He rounded the corner of the house and had to catch himself so as not to trip over a body. A hatless dead man who looked to be in his thirties lay on his side, shot three times in the chest. Damn, who were the gun-crazy wild bastards who did this?

Where were the other ranch hands? He raised his gaze to the log building that looked like the bunkhouse. What would he find in there? In long strides he crossed the open ground and stopped in the doorway.

Two men were strung up between the bunks. Their hands were tied on the top post and they hung from their bound hands with their legs wide apart. The younger man raised up his face and said, "Oh, thank God."

In seconds, Slocum cut him down and eased him to the floor. "Sorry. I better get him down too."

"Sure. Is Roy over there alive?" The youth began rubbing his wrists, no doubt trying to get the feeling back in his hands.

"I think so." After cutting the older man's bindings, Slocum set him up against the bed, and the man acted somewhat recovered.

"I'm Denny," the boy said, stripping the rest of the bindings off his wrists.

"Slocum is my name."

"What about Mrs. Farley?"

"She's alive."

"Oh, my God. They—they—did they—?"

Slocum nodded. "Yes. And much more, I am certain. But she'll recover."

"You seen Calvin?"

"There's a man who was shot down beside the house. They shot the dogs too. Who were they?"

"Drovers, huh, Roy?"

"No-good sonsabitches." The man got onto his knees, bent over the bed and folded his hands to pray aloud. "Dear God, help us catch them and make them pay for what they done. I know I ain't worthy of much, but give me the strength,

Lord, to find them and make them pay for this waste and destruction they've done here. Amen."

"Roy, did you know any of them?" Slocum asked.

Head down in defeat, Roy shook his head. "They were drovers, all right. Crazy, like mad dogs turned loose by someone."

"What else do you recall about them?" Slocum waited for Roy to answer.

"Mexican spur rowels on their boots. They were all acting rabid. One they called Mike. Another they called Lester." Roy pounded his fist on the floor. "Horace. They called the fat one Horace."

"Bridges was the boss," Denny said and rubbed his jaw. "Mean sumbitch busted me with something in his fist."

"Probably had a roll of coins in his fist. Four of them in the gang that you saw?" Slocum looked from one to the other. "Four, huh?"

"There might have been another." Roy looked across at Denny. "Do you think there were five of them when they rode up?"

Denny dropped his chin. "I ain't sure, Roy. That Bridges hit me and the lights went out for a long while."

"Think hard, boys," Slocum said, anger rising in his chest over this whole attack. "I'm going to run them down in the ground, and if there were five here last night, I want the last one too."

Looking done in, the two nodded at him.

"I'll go see if Mrs. Farley's dressed." Slocum rose to his feet. "We'll fix some food. That cow needs to be milked, and the horses need some hay tossed to them."

"We can handle that," Denny said. Roy struggled up to his feet and agreed.

"I'm sorry. I should have come yesterday."

"Chances are if you had, you'd be like Calvin—dead," Roy mumbled.

At the house, Slocum found Mrs. Farley dressed, making coffee and breakfast. He stopped in the doorway. "I'm Charley's friend Slocum."

She turned and then nodded. "I thought so. Come in. Are they—?"

"Roy and Denny are going to be all right. Calvin's dead."

"Thank God those two are all right, at least. Roy was so upset. I feared for him. They shot the dogs—they shot Calvin—" She broke off and began chewing on her lower lip.

Slocum was beside her and hugged her shoulder. "Easy. We're alive. They'll pay for what they did."

"I know. I know, and I hate it."

"No, God has a plan for you."

"I sure hope he does. I've been considering suicide since they left last night. I'd at least be with Charley and Calvin."

"Don't talk like that." He pulled her around and she buried her face in his chest. "People care about you. They need you. Charley never gave up."

"If only he was here."

"How can I help you with breakfast? Those men are starved. We'll have the chores caught up here shortly."

"Oh, Slocum, Charley said you were the man we needed."

"I know. I know. I couldn't have come any faster."

"Oh, I don't blame you—"

"The boys are coming. I hear them."

"We can talk later."

He agreed. The fury inside him boiled. Who were these bastards? Who had made this raid? They'd rue the day they ever rode into that place.

Barr sat up in bed. It was the middle of the night. Who was outside shouting? He glanced over at Erma, who was in a fetal position beside him and shaking in fear.

"Get out here, Barr!" someone in the yard shouted.

Who was doing the shouting? "Hold your damn horses."

"We'll hold your horses. Get your ass out here."

His pants on, he strapped on his gun belt and started for the front door.

"Oh, be careful," Erma moaned after him.

Dumb girl. He opened the front door and peered out into the night. Two steps more and a gun muzzle stuck him in his back. Someone jerked Barr's own six-gun out of the holster.

"We need more money for that job we did on that widow. We're going to have to shag out of here."

"What job?"

"That Farley bitch you wanted run off."

Had they killed her? "How much more?"

"Five hundred apiece."

"Hell, I don't have that much money here."

"Open the gawdamn safe and count it out or you'll be answering to the law with us."

"What happened down there?" he asked the man behind him who'd taken his gun.

"We had to kill one of her men."

"Oh, hell. I told Doss I didn't want anyone killed—"

"We can't help that. But we raped her ass off like you said."

With the gun barrel in his back, he was forced to go inside. Where was Doss? Would he come to Barr's aid?

"Open the safe. We ain't got all night," the leader ordered as he came busting inside the house to take charge.

There was a loaded .30-caliber pistol in the safe. If Barr could get his hands on it, those two would be dead. He intended to send them both to hell. All he had wanted was for them to rape her ass off. They said they shot one of her men? They had really botched a simple deal, and he needed to be rid of them.

On his knees and shaking, Barr soon dialed the safe's combination. When it was unlocked at last, he turned the latch in the flickering candlelight and drew the thick door open. It swung toward the bossy one, the guy they called

Bridges. There on the shelf, Barr could see the small, polished walnut grips of the .30-caliber Colt. All he had to do was draw it out, cock and fire the muzzle in Bridges's face.

But when he reached for the revolver, Bridges used his boot to slam the thick door shut hard, smashing Barr's right arm. The last thing Barr remembered was the two outlaws cursing and beating his head in with their pistol butts.

6

The burial of Calvin Howard at sundown was not an easy one for Slocum. They laid both stock dogs in the grave with him since they said he liked them so much. Supported by her two ranch hands, Minnie Farley took the loss hard and cried through the entire service. Slocum tried to make the ceremony short and comforting, but she'd been through so much there was no raising her above her sorrow.

"Dear Lord, take this man, Calvin Howard, in the palm of your hand and protect him. He was an honest man who gave his life for the others here. In Jesus' name . . . amen"

"Amen."

"If you don't mind, Slocum, I'll cover him up. Calvin made a ranch hand out of me," Denny, the youth of maybe eighteen or so, said. "Be my way to pay him back."

"You handle it."

Minnie kissed first Denny on the cheek, next Roy by squeezing his face in her palms, and then she took Slocum's arm and, lifting her skirt hem in the other hand, they went back to the house. The sun had bled itself down in the west, and twilight had turned the world to gray. Somewhere a coyote howled. Another answered. Nighttime and the crickets set in.

"You can't ever replace men like Charley or Calvin. They didn't make many of them. My first husband, Ethan, was killed down in Colorado in a horse accident. I knew I'd never find another man like him. Charley came along and filled his boots, but—it wasn't the same." Wet-eyed, she looked over at Slocum. "I loved Charley Farley and miss him to this day, but he never was Ethan either. Good as he was to me, it's never the same is it?"

"No. You can look and search, but they'll all be different. Have different points you like, but they're all new patterns."

"You have no wife?" She swept inside the house, blowing her nose.

"Never married."

She turned to look back at him. "No roots either?"

"Severed them all years ago, what with the war and other things."

"Charley told me you had a past that haunted you, and he wondered if you could come."

"That letter finally ran me down." Even through her ravaged face, red from her sorrow and past trials, he saw the beauty in Minnie's strong features that no doubt had attracted a dedicated bachelor like Charley. Her head-high posture and the way she carried herself, even to the twist of her honey brown hair that fell to her shoulders, made her an attractive woman. A swift brush had restored the shine to her hair since he'd had his first sight of her.

"I'm sorry I came too late."

"That's ridiculous. How could you know what happened out here or who planned it?" She busied herself rattling dishes and plates, taking them from the table. At last she turned with her backside against the dry sink and her hands behind her on the tabletop, bracing herself.

"You know what that damned Bridges told me last

night? That if I didn't sell out and leave, he'd be back to do it all over again."

"Who wants you out of here that bad?" Slocum sat astraddle a high-back kitchen chair and studied her for the answer.

"Udall Barr."

"This Bridges ever mention Barr as the one who sent him?"

Her breasts rose and fell under the dress top as she breathed harder. "No, but who else wants my place? He sent that weasel from the bank, Toothacker, out here to offer me twenty bucks a head for my mother cows and two thousand for the land. Damnit, I own four sections of this land. That's not even a dollar an acre."

"You won a water suit in court against Barr?"

"Yes, we did, and the son of a bitch shot Charley—or had Charley shot—over it. I hated that."

"Not your fault. Charley knew what he was up against." Slocum's forehead dropped to rest against the top rung of the ladder chair. "They simply caught him off guard is all."

"Still, they shot him in the back."

Slocum raised his forehead off the ladder chair and looked at her. "Minnie, would you move into town until this is settled?"

"No, I'm not going anywhere, except to see those four and Barr get what they've got coming."

He'd figured as much. But Denny and Roy would be no match for the likes of this Bridges and his men if they returned. And the rapists certainly could ride back that evening and do it all over again and leave no witnesses. A no-win situation.

Minnie used both of her hands to carry the large kettle from the range and pour the steaming water into her dishpan. Then she shaved some soap off a bar into the hot water and began scouring her dishes and utensils with a rag.

Slocum rose, refilled the kettle from the well bucket and

set it back on the stove top. Using a lid lifter, he looked inside and then fed the low fire some fresh kindling. Kettle in place, he folded his arms over his chest, still in a quandary over what he should do about her safety.

"This sure ain't your first job at cooking." She laughed. A melodic sound he'd not heard before from her, almost like a teenage girl all wound up at a dance.

"I've done my share. Lost a camp cook one time going to Kansas with a herd. He drowned crossing Crooked Hammer Creek. We tried five different drovers at being the cook, and before my hands all quit out there on that prairie and went back home, I put out the grub the rest of the way."

"I can just see you in a white apron ringing the triangle." She shook her head as if to clear it and laughed again. "I'll remember if I ever need a camp cook to call on Slocum."

"I may be hard of hearing by then."

He went to the doorway and listened to the night, which had fallen while he and Minnie had talked in the kitchen. The sound of Denny's shovel rang each time he scooped up more dirt and gravel. Slocum could see the glow of Roy's roll-your-own when he drew on it as he squatted close by the grave-filling operation.

Then the shoveling stopped and Denny took out a mouth harp and began to play. Roy took up the shovel and went to using it. The strains of Denny's harmonica filled the night with "Nearer, My God, to Thee."

As Denny played the hymn, Slocum mouthed the words that he knew so well from his youth sitting on the church pews. Then he heard Minnie join in.

"Nearer, my God, to Thee, nearer to Thee! E'en though it be a cross that raiseth me, still all my song shall be, nearer, my God, to Thee. Nearer, my God, to Thee, nearer to Thee."

Before they finished the hymn, Minnie came over to stand beside him and squeezed his arm.

"That was sweet and dear," she said. "Calvin's been properly laid to rest tonight." With a knot in his throat that he couldn't swallow, Slocum agreed with a nod.

By the time they got him close to North Platte, Barr felt that his wild ride to the doctor's in the back of the buckboard was worse than the beating at the hands of the gang. His foreman, Doss, and Erma lathered the team hard making the run. Lying on his back in a bedroll on the floor of the buckboard with his bloody head wrapped in torn-up sheets, Barr was tossed and bounced until at last he told them to slow down.

Strong arms carried him up the stairs to the doctor's office. After being placed on an examining table, he watched the doctor hook his gold-framed glasses behind his ears, and then Barr fainted.

He roused again briefly just in time to hear, ". . . he's going to lose half his left ear. . . ."

"Will he live?"

"Of course he'll live. He's a stout individual. He simply won't be as pretty."

Then Barr's world dissolved back into darkness.

He awoke like a drowning man. What day was it? Erma jumped up from her nearby chair and moved to his side. Morning sunshine slanted in a bright shaft from the open window. His left arm was in a sling. How damn long had he been here? Then he moved his head to see more, and the pain struck him like a bolt of lightning. What had they done to him?

"Here," she said and held a tablespoon of medicine out to him. "Doctor said to give you some if you woke up. It's for the pain."

He raised up enough to sip it. It tasted bad.

"Did Doss and the men go look for that son of a bitch?" His own voice, even in a whisper, sounded rusty and cracked. "You just remember that they wore masks and we didn't know them."

She nodded that she knew what to say and gave him the rest of the laudanum. His head back on the pillow, he could hardly wait for it to take effect. It soon did and he was off again.

When he awoke the next time, he could hear them talking—Erma and, he thought, the sheriff.

"No. I was so scared—I never noticed anything. It was at night. I heard them in there swearing at him, and then they beat him half to death after he opened the safe for them."

"I'm sorry, Miss Erma. I need more information. Did any of Barr's men notice anything about them that you know of?"

"No, some of the other gang members held them in the bunkhouse."

"Then they knew your operation. Could they have been men that used to work for Barr?"

"They wore masks. I don't know. I've only worked there a short while."

"Any idea about how much money they got?"

"They cleaned out the safe. All the money that he had—"

Barr closed his eyes. *You done good, girl.*

7

Slocum prepared to leave the Farley ranch the next morning. He told Minnie, Roy and Denny to remain armed and close. He suggested that Denny climb the windmill tower several times a day and use Charley's binoculars to look over the country, and that they all three should stay in the main house at night; meanwhile he'd try to get a lead on the gang.

Buck short-loped most of the way to North Platte. Clouds were gathering in the southwest. He expected rain by late afternoon, when the towering clouds got tall enough to wring it out. Rain wouldn't hurt them. Might even help folks' fresh-planted fall gardens of cabbage and turnips.

He reached town in midmorning. At the jail, he found Garner's chief deputy, Sam Welch, who told him about Barr. "The boss is over at the doc's office now talking to Barr's farm girl, Erma, about the gang. All Barr's men would say was that the men were masked and they caught them all off guard."

"How many men?"

"Four or five. Why?"

"That many men attacked Minnie Farley earlier that night.

49

They shot and killed one of her men, a Calvin—" Slocum shook his head. "I can't recall his last name. Then they tied her to the bed, took turns raping her and told her to get out or they'd be back and do it again."

"Oh, God, Slocum, who were they?" Welch looked sickened by the news.

"The ringleader was a guy called Bridges."

The deputy narrowed his left eye. "Big Texan, a troublemaker. I ain't seen him in town today."

"What about a Horace somebody? A fat guy."

"He's Bridges's shadow."

"Where do they stay?"

"They've got a camp along the Platte River west of town. Tents and corrals is all, squatting on some river land in them willows."

"I may ride out there and have a look around."

"Be careful." Welch shook his head. "I'd go with you, but I better watch the town, with Huey working on the Barr case and all."

"I understand." Slocum turned on his heels.

"Better take one of these shotguns. You may need it up there." Welch fumbled with the keys to open one of the locks in the chain to get a shotgun for him. "I always like them in close range."

"Won't hurt." Slocum broke open the breech of the double-barreled Greener. It was clean as a whistle, and when he snapped it back shut, he smiled. The damn British made some great shotguns.

Welch handed him a handful of high brass, twelve-gauge cartridges. "Twelve number two buckshot to the shell."

"That should stop anyone."

"I wish to hell that I could go—"

Slocum dismissed his offer. "They've probably rode on already."

"Be damn careful. If they're as bad as I think they are, you need to shoot first and ask questions later."

Slocum agreed.

After getting a crude map from Welch, Slocum thanked the man and went outside to mount Buck. There was no sign of the sheriff, so he headed Buck west. Lots of wagon and horse tracks cut through the sandy river overflow ground making up the pencil-marked road on Welch's map. Places where rigs had bottomed out, the road swung around or had been built up with cut brush thrown in to fill the sinkhole.

Lots of poor folks squatted in the river bottoms. Crate shacks, canvas strung on crooked poles, women in wash-worn dresses stared at him as a stranger passing by. Others puffed on corncob pipes and snubbed him, rocking in their weathered gray rockers. Their sisters hung dull wet clothing on bushes and called their children back like they were venturesome pups—curious about the invader on the jogging dun horse with a shotgun across his lap.

Short of the camp, he reined up Buck and broke open the Greener. He loaded it with shells from his vest pocket, then snapped the barrel shut one-handed and pushed Buck on. He could smell wood smoke, and once around the brush screen, he saw two women bolt up from cooking something and eye him critically.

"This the Bridges camp?" He noted that there were only two horses in the pens, and they looked gaunt. Not the kind of mounts that a man like Bridges would ride.

The harder-looking woman swept some gray-streaked hair back from her face. "Who's asking? You the damn law?"

"I'm looking for Bridges."

"Well, gawdamn you, tough guy, get off your horse and look for yourself. The sumbitch ain't here."

"When did you see him last?"

"I asked—"

"Personally, I'm not interested in your mouth. Where's Bridges?"

"How should I know?"

"He lives here, doesn't he?"

She shrugged. "Tell him, Terry."

The plain-looking girl with a belly full of baby straining her thin dress shook her head. "They never tell us anything. We're just their slaves, and Lincoln turned them all free—right?"

"I heard that he did. When was the last time they were here?"

"Yesterday."

"Much obliged." He touched the shotgun barrel to his hat brim and started to turn Buck around.

"Hold up," the older woman said. "You didn't ride down here for nothing. What did they do to you?"

"Killed a man and raped a widow woman."

"Where?" She hurried over, carrying her old dress hem high and exposing her skinny calves.

"West of town."

"Why didn't the real law come 'stead of you?"

"I came to kill them. All the law would have done is arrested 'em."

She snorted out her nose. "I saw that look in your face when you rode up. Well, you won't catch them. They're too smart for that." Her taunting laughter following after him made the skin draw tight on his cheeks.

Others had thought that too. *But, lady, they're all dead.*

Back in town, he returned the shotgun and spoke to Sheriff Garner before he rode out of North Platte. Garner left him wondering about the four or so masked men who had robbed Barr. Something wasn't right. Neither he nor the sheriff felt that they knew half enough about the crime—it was all sounding too vague to Slocum.

In the doc's office, Barr sat up bare assed on the bed, and Erma jumped up to steady him so he could rise and pee in the enamel bucket at his feet. How much money did they get out of his safe? Five to seven thousand—he'd not counted the total amount lately. That sumbitch Bridges. Doss better have found him and them others by this time and got the biggest part of the money back or he'd hang Doss's ass too.

Finished emptying his bladder, Barr dropped his butt on the bed, and Erma squatted down to put the pot back underneath the cot.

"No word?" he asked under his breath.

"No word." Erma halfway rose and then backed into her chair.

There was no way for him to send *her* out to learn anything. He needed to be healed and chasing down that Bridges himself. Why, the SOB was probably headed for Mexico with all that money and busy planning to have a high old time below the border at Barr's expense. If he ever caught Bridges, he'd smash his balls with a hammer, one at a time, for what he did to scar Barr's head. Half of his fucking left ear was all he had left. He looked like some steer on a ranch in Kansas who'd been through five owners in his life. Jaws clamped, he ground his back teeth together, and that hurt too.

The damn sheriff had been here, and Barr had told him all that he dared. His head on the pillow, he couldn't sleep on his left side because of the injured ear. Oh, he'd get Bridges, and that bastard would rue the day he'd robbed him and left him for dead on the floor.

Erma drove Barr home the next day. Nothing improved his disposition, not even the good whiskey she'd bought for him. Barr was half drunk when he got there, and Mozelle and Erma had to pack him inside the house. He passed out and slept for twelve hours.

8

After talking to Sheriff Garner, Slocum swung by Leta's tent. She came out from behind the flap wrapped in a housecoat to greet him. Her hand shaded her eyes against the midday glare as she looked up at him seated on his horse. "What are you doing?"

"Looking for some rapists."

"Who?" She made a serious frown.

"A Texan named Bridges."

"Watch him. He's mean as a prairie rattler."

Slocum nodded that he'd heard her. "Bridges may have robbed Barr that night too."

"Might?"

"Barr told the sheriff that the ones who robbed him, and who also pistol-whipped him, were all masked."

"Get down. I'll make some coffee."

"I better get back. I figure Bridges has taken a shuck of the country, and I'm going to try and find him."

"Be careful. He usually keeps a gang."

"He had them with him at her place."

"Farley's widow?"

Slocum nodded. "They also gunned down one of her men."

Standing beside him and his horse, she slapped his leg. "You're going after them all by yourself, huh?"

He nodded. "I'll be back. Is the lumber coming?"

"Yes," A smile crossed her mouth. "It should be here this week."

"Good luck," he said, then waved and turned Buck off. Too damn tempting for him to get off and be with her, but things needed to be done. He short-loped back to Minnie's ranch.

Both of her men, armed with rifles, met him at the corral.

"What did you learn?" Denny asked.

"Let's tell it all to Minnie too. She all right?"

They nodded and headed for the house. Minnie met them in the doorway in a fresh white apron. "Coffee's made. Come on in."

When they were all seated at the table, she filled their cups.

Slocum told them all about the Barr robbery and what he knew about the subject of Barr's beating.

"You figure that was Bridges and his gang?" Denny asked.

"Barr kept saying to the sheriff that they were masked. But in fact, when I questioned Sheriff Garner, he wondered if they really were masked."

"What does that mean?" Minnie asked.

"Makes one wonder, doesn't it?" Slocum blew on his coffee to cool it enough to drink.

Standing across the table from him, she wet her lips. "Do you think Bridges left the country?"

"Yes."

"Good. What will you do?"

"I'm going to swing south and see if I can cut his trail."

Her face melted into one of concern. "By yourself?"

"There isn't any posse going to do a thing. I may or may not get a line on where he's headed."

"Don't waste your life for me. I'll live the rest of my life all right."

He nodded that he'd heard her. "People like Bridges don't stop hurting folks until someone stops them."

"But—"

"I may need to borrow a packhorse."

"Sure," she said. "We'll pick you out a good one." The men agreed with sharp nods.

"Good. I'll head out in the morning."

"Could I go along?" Denny asked.

"If Bridges is out of the country, I guess I could hire some more men in town," Minnie said.

"Better keep your job," Slocum said to the young man.

"I can find another. I'll miss her and Roy, but I want to help you find them."

Minnie refilled the coffee cups around the table. "Denny and Calvin were close friends. I can see why he wants to help find Calvin's killer."

Slocum nodded. "It sure won't be any Sunday school picnic."

Denny agreed. "I know, but I can help—someway."

"You own a horse?" Slocum asked.

"He can take one of mine," Minnie said.

"All right. We leave before dawn." Slocum shook his head in dismay that he'd agreed to it and then blew on his fresh coffee. All he needed was a green kid along with him—time would tell.

Before sunup the next morning, they rode out. Slocum wanted to make a big circle to see if he could detect any direction the rapists had gone after they'd left Minnie's place and, more than likely, after they'd robbed and pistol-whipped Barr.

"Tracking down men like Bridges is never easy. This is a big country, and there's lots of places for them to hide."

Slocum rode stirrup to stirrup with Denny, who was coming along with the stout packhorse that carried their bedrolls and some camp things Minnie'd loaned them.

"Where do you think he'll go?"

"Maybe Texas. But I figure he's wanted down there for something."

"Where does that leave him to go?"

"No telling." Slocum twisted in the saddle to look back over his shoulder. Nothing but waving grass and rolling country behind them. There was a trading post south of North Platte on the Texas Trail that skirted the Kansas ban on cattle drives and came up the east side of Colorado. Wilbur's Store and Saloon was a raw example of frontier commerce on the wet side of the line. Kansas prohibition drove drinkers out of state to quench their thirst. This would be the place Bridges might have first stopped on his way to escape.

"You ever been to Wilbur's?" Slocum asked.

Denny nodded. "Tough place. Calvin and I came up here with a herd two years ago. We laid over there for two days to let the cattle recover some. They shot one of our cowboys and another Mexican got knifed to death in those two days. There's a cemetery out back with so many fresh graves it looks like a prairie dog town."

"You've sure been there."

"What do we have to do when we get there?"

A red-tailed hawk sailed over them, screaming in protest at their invasion. Slocum smiled at its flight. "Keep our wits. Stay out of the way of anyone wanting a fight and try to learn about Bridges—if he came through here is all we need to know. Oh, if he or one of his men dropped any information about where they're headed, it would be nice to know that too."

"You don't expect to learn that, then?" Denny laughed.

"We sure need it though. Any lead would be good."

"Like a spark to start a fire, huh?"

"A spark would be nice." Be damned nice. They'd reach Wilbur's by sundown. It would be their first chance to learn if the gang had gone through there.

Slocum dismounted short of the hitch rack and handed his reins to Denny. "I'll go look around. Stay mounted till I come out."

Denny nodded and took their horses aside.

Out of habit, Slocum felt for his holster and adjusted it crossing the open ground. There were a dozen jaded, salt dried, hip shot horses at the racks. *Rode hard and put away wet.* He passed them, not seeing a familiar brand, but he had no idea what brand the rapists' horses might bear.

Inside the dark barroom, dimly lit by flickering candle power, the strong smell of horse, sweat and deeper fecal odors filled his nose. He looked over the room's occupants and drew some squint-eyed stares back from some of them at the side tables. But no one moved out of place. He went to the end of the bar with the wall to his back and ordered a beer.

The barrel-chested bartender carried two small-caliber pistols in a red sash around his great girth and three big knives that Slocum could count. He hadn't shaved in a long time, and under his wild, bushy eyebrows his eyes looked like polished coal.

"What ya be wanting? Food? Women?"

"A beer."

He took the dime Slocum paid him. "What else?"

"Four men came through here in the last twenty-four hours—one called himself Bridges, another was big as a bear. Horace was his name."

"What ya be needing them fur?"

"Rape and murder."

"Them's tough charges." The man looked Slocum up and down. "You'd make a match fur them. Yeah, they rode on south."

"How long ago?"

"Ah, be this morning they did that."

"Did they mention where they were going?"

"Frizzy, get your ass over here." He waved a big ham of an arm at a young whore working on some guy in a chair.

"What'cha need me for?" she asked, coming over and eyeing Slocum like a fat stock buyer.

"He'll pay you a dollar to tell him where that last customer you had was going." The big man turned back to Slocum. "Put'cher money where your mouth is at, mister."

Slocum obeyed.

"Cold Springs."

"Where's Cold Springs?"

"Fuck if I know." She shrugged her thin bare shoulders. "He said, 'Boys, let's go to Cold Springs.'"

Slocum motioned for her to take the money and turned to the barkeep. "You ever hear of Cold Springs? I know where Colorado Springs is, but Cold Springs is a new one on me."

The big man, who stank like a boar hog, delivered his beer. "She told you what she knew."

"They mention Texas?"

"They didn't say shit to me. Got two bottles of whiskey. That Bridges paid for 'em and that big guy wanted some pussy, so he took Frizzy on. The rest got loaded drunk and finally stormed out of here. That's all I know, mister. When the law comes by, who should I tell 'em was here?"

"Tell them that Slocum was here looking for 'em."

"And I'll do that, but the only law comes by here are the deputy U.S. marshals, and they're looking for bootleggers."

Slocum finished his beer, thanked the man and went out the batwing doors. He paused on the porch to let his eyes adjust to the brightness. Another puncher came outside and spit tobacco juice off the porch.

"You looking for Cold Springs?" He wiped off his mouth on the back of his hand.

Slocum nodded.

"It's southwest from here, maybe two days' hard riding. The water ain't cold either. I been there."

"Trading post outfit?"

"Yeah."

Slocum fished out another silver dollar from his vest. He tossed it to the man. "We'll find it."

"What's that?" Denny asked, riding up and handing Slocum the reins to Buck.

"Cold Springs. You ever been there?"

"Nope."

"I guess by tomorrow or the next day you'll know all about it."

Denny blinked at him. "That's where they went?"

"A whore inside heard them say that's where they were going."

"What did all that cost?"

"Two dollars and a dime. And I got a warm beer to boot and all that information." In the saddle, Slocum started out in a trot. "Let's make tracks. They ain't that far ahead."

He hoped, anyway.

There was no rest for Barr. When Doss came back empty-handed, he threw a raging fit. "Those bastards took seven thousand dollars out of my safe, and you can't find them?"

"Boss, they ain't in the country, and no one knows if they went north or south. I really got after that woman who says she's his wife. All she said was that big bastard called Slocum asked her where he was too."

"Where's he at now?"

"I don't know. He don't seem to be in town or anywhere close."

"Take two men and a pack outfit and you go find his trail. He's after Bridges because of what they did to his buddy's wife. Let him take Bridges on, then you step in, eliminate him and get my money back."

"Hell, they might ride to Texas."

"I don't care where they ride to. You get that done. Saddle some fresh horses. Get you two tough men to ride along with you and go find that fucking Slocum. Be sure he finds Bridges before you turn your hand. Savvy?"

"What if he don't find him?"

"Don't come back— No, that guy will find Bridges. Send me telegrams of where you're at. But code them."

"What do you mean?"

"Use words like 'Saw your aunt today.'"

"What does that mean?"

"Means you saw Slocum."

"Call him your aunt?" Doss looked upset.

"Yeah." Simple enough, even Doss should understand.

"All right, I'll go look for him, but I don't think it'll work."

"It better work. That was all the money I had to survive on, do you understand?"

"Yeah, I know, but I can't think where to even start looking."

"Bridges rode out. How did you learn that Slocum rode out after him?"

"Talk in the Texas Moon Saloon. A guy said Slocum'd been by there looking for Bridges. He figured that Slocum was going— Oh—no. No, it was a deputy sheriff told the bartender he figured that Slocum was going after them for what they did to Mrs. Farley."

"Slocum's the guy came to town asking about Farley?"

"That was the word. Them two were old buddies. They also said him and Leta Couzki are old friends too."

"You ask her?"

"Naw. She ain't working the damn saloons anymore. She's building herself a brand-new whorehouse."

"Maybe you ought to squeeze the information out of her as to where he went. Gawdamnit, Doss, I hired you to do these things. You said that Bridges would handle the job of screwing the ass off Mrs. Farley, no problem. Well, he got us in a worse fix, and she's still over there."

"I never thought—"

"That's the truth. Now run down this Slocum, then let him take Bridges and you scoop up the rest."

"All right. I'm getting supplies and leaving. Don't know when I'll be back."

"Just find them."

"I'll try, I'll try."

With Doss gone, Barr dropped heavily into his leather chair. His damn ear hurt and the headache was back, pounding in both sides of his head. No way he could ride after that bunch—he felt so helpless. He took some laudanum and soon stumbled off to bed and fell back asleep.

For two days Barr did nothing much but rest and take medicine for the pain in his head. The second day after Doss left, Barr was sitting in his leather chair when Mozelle came into the room and stood next to him. "I think Erma is pregnant. She's sick every morning. What should I do?"

Damn, it sure hadn't taken long to get her knocked up. "In the morning you take her up to Doc Crawford and have him get rid of it."

"He'll charge ten dollars."

"I'll give you the money." Crawford kept an office over by Chenneyville. If someone wanted to be treated for anything, they had to go see him in the morning, 'cause by evening he was too drunk to do shit. He made most all of his money ending unwanted pregnancies.

Barr shook his head—one more damn problem. "Get me some more medicine. My head's killing me."

The woman agreed and went after some laudanum for him.

That night in bed, Barr worked Erma's ass over good. She'd probably be too sore for a few days to do anything after Crawford got through with her. When Barr finished

with her for the night, he rolled over on his side and wondered what Doss was doing out there. He might just shoot
his damn foreman if he didn't find Slocum and Bridges this
time. At the moment, he needed that money, and badly.

9

The sun was setting fast on day two for Slocum and Denny. They made a dry camp out on the prairie. With his hat cocked back, Denny Kline sat cross-legged on the ground beside Slocum. The small fire's glow radiated off his smooth forehead as they fed their faces with frijoles from tin plates. Slocum asked him where he came from.

"I was raised in a whorehouse in East Texas. Woman who said she birthed me was Thelma Kline. She worked there. Said I was the cause of that—why she worked in such a place. Said she and a young man named Hampton Orwell were pledged to get married. He got hisself kilt in a knife fight over on the Louisiana line. When her pa found out she was going to have me, he threw her out and shunned her.

"So when I was fourteen I run off. I stopped an old man to ask if I could work out a meal for myself, and he made me his slave. When I got a chance I cut out on him. Course he said I stole his horse. But I worked my ass off for him and he owed me six months' wages—the damn horse wasn't that good.

"I got hooked up with Calvin Howard in Fort Worth. He took a liking to me and got me on as a cook's helper on a trail drive. We took them cattle to Dodge City, Kansas. Next year I was a full-fledged drover, and we went around them damn Kansas farmers and up the trail back over there that they called the Texas Trail.

"When we got to North Platte, Calvin found Charley Farley and we both got on with him. Been there two years. Calvin showed me everything. How to use a gun. How to fix a saddle. I can shoe horses. And I can rope with rest of them."

"Sounds like he was the father you never had," Slocum said.

"He was. He was—and I get teary eyed every time thinking about them bastards killing him."

Slocum took the empty plate from him and, on his knees, refilled it from the kettle. "I can understand that. Eat some more. In a few days, maybe even tomorrow, we're going have us a meeting with them bastards and settle that score."

"You think they killed Mr. Farley?"

"No telling, but if Minnie'd been my widow and Charley was still alive, I'd sure hope Charley would have taken up their tracks. He would have. He was that kind of a guy."

"Why is it the good guys get killed and these worthless outfits are still breathing?"

"I don't try to figure out God's ways, but you're right. Some miserable men are alive and some good ones gone."

"You think this bunch will put up a big fight when we catch them?"

Slocum sat back on his butt and nodded. "Wouldn't you? If there was a posse on your tail and you figured out that they intended to either shoot you or hang you?"

"Damn right, I would."

"There's your answer." For Slocum, Denny had filled in lots of information about his upbringing and also his dedication to his dead mentor.

"We were going to try and start a ranch in a few years."

"Well, you'll make that," Slocum said. "It may take a little longer."

"Yeah," Denny said and scrambled up for the coffeepot. "But I'm going to do it."

Slocum held up his cup for more.

A coyote cut loose out in the night and yapped for the rest of them. Soon others cut in. They obviously were closing in for a kill of some unfortunate prey. Slocum wished that he and Denny were as sure of their own hunt and closing in on the gang.

He blew on the steam. The coffee was too hot to drink. The warm moisture softened the beard stubble around his mouth. He could sure use a bath and a shave. There might be time for that later.

The next day, they were in the saddle before the purple first light of dawn and heading southwest across the bunchgrass-and-sagebrush rolling country. A coolness penetrated Slocum's clothing that reminded him fall wasn't far away. By the time the sun was up they'd bake again, but the shorter days and all pointed at fall sweeping down out of the Canadian provinces.

They found a low-roofed cabin, logs dark with age and the corral rails long sun-bleached. A couple of dogs barked at their approach, a sure sign they would find residents.

Short of the front door, Slocum reined up and started to get off his horse. A man with a shotgun came to the door. With teeth bared behind his snowy beard, he spoke, his voice sounding high-pitched.

"That's close enough."

"We aren't going to harm you. We're looking for Cold Springs."

"You two look like the class of scoundrels that they entertain. Keep riding southeast. It's still down there."

Slocum nodded. "Thanks for your hospitality."

He remounted. *Strange old man's been out there too long by himself.* With a salute of his hat brim, Slocum reined Buck around and they rode on.

Denny looked back. "He was sure unfriendly. Hell, all we wanted was directions."

"Folks go a little mad living way out by themselves for too long."

"I'll remember that. Tell me: Weren't you worried about that shotgun?"

"He never had it cocked, or I'd have forgotten about asking him anything."

Denny laughed. "He sure made me uncomfortable-feeling as all hell."

Slocum checked behind and saw nothing but the rolling country. Trotting their horses, they kept on course, eventually reaching an east-west wagon road that looked well used.

"I figure this is the road we need. If we haven't ridden past it, Cold Springs should be ahead of us."

Denny agreed. They watered their animals at a small, sluggish creek that snaked through the sandy stream bottom. Then they rode on, crossing a tall ridge, and at the base was a line of tall cottonwoods, and smoke from cooking fires swirled out of them. Several tall tepees stood to one side. Slocum could see some Indian women wrapped in blankets moving around the camp. Small brown children ran about playing with black and yellow cur dogs.

"It's an Injun camp," Denny said, looking around warily. "They on the warpath?"

"No. The women and children being here, I'd say it's a peaceful place."

"Good."

The noisy, playing youngsters grew silent when they noticed the two riders and packhorse coming toward them. Their dark eyes watched the two riders with deep suspicion as they passed by.

"You seen any trading post yet?" Denny stood in the stirrups and looked around.

"I figure that it's here somewhere."

They rode on alongside the shallow, murky-looking creek underneath the gnarled trees that lined the waterway. Coin-sized leaves twirled overhead, stirred by the strong wind. A cluster of low-walled sod buildings and pole corrals soon appeared. Slocum reined up his horse. He needed to alert the kid that this might be the place where all hell broke loose.

"From here on keep your wits about you. If they recognize either of us, there may be gunplay."

"I've been thinking along those lines too."

"You know what these men look like. So clear your throat if you recognize them."

"There ain't no saddle stock around." Denny twisted in the saddle in search of them.

"We'll hitch our horses and go inside anyway. They may have pushed on already."

A few flickering candles cast a weak yellow light on the room when Slocum opened the door. A white-bearded man behind the counter met his gaze when Slocum ducked under the hand-hacked-out lintel to enter.

"Howdy."

Slocum nodded that he heard him and searched in the shadowy room for sight of anyone else. Nothing moved. There was no one else there. Damn, they'd missed them after all that hard riding.

"Can I help you gents?" the storekeeper asked.

"We're looking for four men." Slocum walked over to the counter and faced the man.

"You a U.S. marshal?"

Slocum shook his head. "Denny and I are looking for four rapists and killers. They raped his boss lady and shot his best friend."

The man shrugged. "They ain't here."

Slocum put a silver dollar on the bar. "Have they been here?"

"Maybe."

Another cartwheel slapped on the bar, and the man frowned at the money. "That ain't enough."

"Next thing I'll do is pistol-whip the story out of you. That's all I'm paying you."

"You want Bridges, huh?"

Slow-like, Slocum nodded at the man across the counter. His anger was rising fast.

"Well, to start with, they ain't here. Rode out this morning."

"Four of them?"

A nod told him the answer, and the man went on, "They wasn't too plain about where they were going next. I took it from the talk they wanted to go back to Texas, but Bridges didn't act like he wanted to go home."

"I suspect there's wanted posters in the Lone Star State for him."

"Maybe."

"I want to buy some food for us to eat and horse grain."

"I can get you some stew. It's fresh made and I've got some shelled corn I'll sell ya."

"Stew first," Slocum said. "We'll put our horses up later."

The two of them took seats at the table with a candle set in the middle in an empty sardine can. The man's half-breed wife served them stew on tin plates with spoons for utensils and hot coffee in tin cans. She was neither pretty nor friendly. Short and potbellied, her long black hair hung limp and tangled in her face.

The storekeeper, who introduced himself as Silas Wickers, joined them. His wife brought him food and coffee too. Slocum considered the pair typical of such isolated places—tough old man who had probably trapped in his younger years. Wickers'd bought her as a teenager from some buck who needed money for whiskey. More Indian than white, the man existed on the far edges of civilization, trading with the red men and passersby.

The meal tasted flat and even some rock salt sprinkled on it didn't liven up the flavor. But Slocum didn't expect much more—some gristly meat and the rest potatoes, rice and beans. The stew would simply fill a void inside him.

"I guess Bridges and his men didn't stay here long?" Slocum turned his ear toward the man for his reply.

"One night was all. You're close behind them."

"Did they grain their horses?"

Wickers shook his face. "They never saw much care either. Left them saddled all the time. I figured they knew that someone was on their back trail."

Denny and Slocum shared a nod.

"They also robbed a big rancher up at North Platte. His men might be coming after them too."

Wickers nodded, using some of the stale bread to sop up the juices on his plate. "Sounds like they were busy rascals. Drank some whiskey and sat around was all they did here. Never talked much aloud. That big guy called Bridges shut them up, and he did all the talking."

"Never mentioned another town or place that they might go next?"

"You know about Fort Supply?"

"Yes, it's a military outpost south of Dodge. North of the Canadian River."

"There was something there. I don't know what, but I did hear them talk about it."

"Thanks," Slocum said and finished the bitter coffee. "We'll be moving on before it gets too dark."

"I've got that shelled corn in fifty-pound sacks. That too much?" Wickers pushed out his chair to get up.

"It'll work." Slocum lofted his can of coffee to finish it off.

"Tell me one thing." Denny wiped his mouth off getting up. "How much do they sell a woman like yours for?"

"A good horse. Why? You want one?" the trader asked.

"Maybe someday. I was just thinking how handy she'd be."

"Come see me. I can get you a pretty one. Not like mine."

"How's that?"

"Aw, the bucks would hang around here all the time if she was pretty. I don't need a good-looking one working here at the store."

Denny nodded and they went to the counter. Slocum paid Wickers. The youth shouldered the sack of corn and they went outside. With the sack fastened on top of the packhorse's load, they rode off. Slocum wasn't planning to sleep around the trading post—safe or unsafe, he was taking no chances. He'd choose the spot. He wanted to be a good distance from the post and the Indians before they bedded down.

"I don't guess he was lying about him finding me a squaw, huh?" Denny unloaded the corn off the top of the packs.

"Probably not." Slocum chuckled. He wasn't certain that Denny would want a squaw for very long. They usually got very demanding and vocal unless you beat them. Slocum had simply parted ways with them when they got too bossy.

"What's so bad about that?" Denny asked.

Slocum took off the canvas cover and folded it. "Nothing, nothing. It sure beats sleeping by yourself."

Denny nodded that it was settled and lifted the left pannier off the sawbucks while Slocum filled the feed bags. The sun was slitting down in the west. Bridges's bunch weren't that far ahead, and on jaded horses they wouldn't make much more distance than Slocum and the boy would trailing them.

Barr's headache pounded in his temples. No one besides him was in the house. Early that morning his housekeeper, Mozelle, had taken Erma to the doctor. He didn't need any baby sucking on her and all that mess. Like a man lost, he roamed the house. His new foreman, Roudy Kelly, and the crew were supposed to be moving other cattle off his range. To escape his headache and sore ear, he took a tablespoon of laudanum—maybe he'd get some relief. Not a damn word from Doss—he'd been gone three days anyway. Not much communication down there where they went in Kansas or Colorado. Still, he needed that money, and pacing the floor wasn't getting it back.

When the painkiller set in enough to halfway numb him so he could think, he saddled his horse and rode for North Platte. Maybe there was a telegram at the wire office from Doss. Hell, he should have gone with him. He blinked his eyes—no way he could have made that long a ride with his persistent headaches. This trip to North Platte was already wearing him out.

He dismounted at the crowded telegraph office and depot. The place swarmed with sodbusters, some newly arrived, sitting on large trunks waiting for transportation. All these bastards needed to be shipped back to where they came from. Speaking foreign languages, they weren't Americans. Them pancake caps they wore looked like dried cow piles to him.

Inside the depot, more women with children and cheap luggage filled the wooden benches. Snotty-nosed brats— they ought to all have been drowned at birth.

"Any wires for Barr?"

"No," the operator under the celluloid visor said to him. "You expecting one?"

"Yes, I am."

"Sorry, Mr. Barr, nothing so far today."

After he left the station and felt better being out of the company of all those honyockers, he rode his horse up to the livery and had him stabled. On the boardwalk, he felt light-headed and rested for a few minutes with his shoulder to the wall outside Hammond's Mercantile.

"Barr!"

Someone in the street was shouting at him. He blinked his eyes and tried to see the man yelling his name. The sun's glare blanked out his view of the rider.

"Barr, if you don't stop chousing my cattle, I'm going to chouse you."

"Who the hell—?"

"I'm Carter Jones of the 7T, and I'm warning you—" Jones's anxious horse spun around under him and he fought him down. "The very next time I catch your men driving any of my cattle, it will be their last."

Barr knew it was no time for him to challenge the son of a bitch. He was so numb he couldn't outdraw anyone's grandmother. Who was this Jones? Nothing fit. He stood unsteady on his boot heels as people went by him on both sides. Good, Jones was riding on. He better find out who Jones was. Damn, he needed to get somewhere and lie down. . . .

He was in the doctor's office on a table when he recovered from his faint. Why was he there?

"I see you're awake," the doctor said, fitting his glasses behind his ears.

"What the hell happened?"

"You passed out down there on the boardwalk, and some husky boys carried you up here."

"What's wrong with me? I don't have any strength."

"You need to go easier. You have lots more to recover from that beating they gave you."

"But I have a ranch to operate—"

"You have to recover first. You better hire the rest of it done."

Unable to keep his eyes open a moment longer, Barr went back to sleep.

10

"Wake up," Slocum whispered to Denny in his bedroll. "We've got company."

"Huh?"

Squatted beside the younger man, Slocum held him down. "Easy. They're trying to steal our horses."

"Who is it?"

With a shake of his head, Slocum raised up with his gun in his fist. He ran low to try to stop the rustlers, who made small targets. Under the starry night sky, there was little light. He could make out a hatless man leading his horse.

"Stop or I'll shoot."

The thief dropped the lead rope and ran toward some cedars. Bullets rang out and Slocum hit the ground. He managed two quick shots at the fleeing figure. Then on his feet again, he raced to catch the one stealing Denny's horse.

His boots churning up dirt, he cut across the landscape, headed for the dry wash. Just in time, he emerged on the bank to leap over and take the rider off Denny's horse. Landing in a breath-busting flop on the ground with the other man underneath him, Slocum quickly gripped his six-gun in his fist and stuck the barrel in his prisoner's face.

"No shoot! No shoot!"

On his feet, Slocum jerked the man up. "Who are you?"

"No hurt me. . . ."

"This one's shot," Denny said from up on top of the bank.

"Your horse is down here." Slocum used the man's collar to drag his prisoner back up the steep bank. "I've got this one."

At the camp, they built up the fire and the two tied-up breeds sat on the ground. The wounded one was only scratched, and he wouldn't die from the injury.

"Who are you?" Slocum asked.

Neither one of them spoke up.

"I'm getting short on patience. Who are you?"

"Me Joe," the uninjured one said. He indicated the wounded one. "Him Bird."

"Who do you work for?"

"No work for anyone."

"You know Bridges?" Slocum folded his arms over his chest and scowled at them.

Joe shook his head.

"Stealing our horses is a crime that will get you hung."

Neither breed showed any emotion.

"You think someone hired them to steal our horses?" Denny asked.

"Damn strange they found us out here and tried to take our horses. Those killers aren't that far ahead of us. Search them. They have any money on them, we'll know, huh?"

"I can do that." Denny pushed Joe over and searched him. He rose and showed Slocum a roll of bills in the firelight. "Where did he earn this?"

Slocum jerked Joe up to his feet and got in his face. "Bridges paid you."

Joe tried to back up, but Slocum's grasp on his shirt kept him confined. "Did he send you to kill us?"

The breed nodded.

With a shove, he dropped the bound prisoner on the ground. "That solves that. Bridges either knows we're back here or suspects we are."

"How could he?" Denny tossed some more wood on the fire.

"Maybe he's guessing. And just making sure no one trails them. He tell you who we were?" Slocum asked Joe.

"He say you killers looking for him."

"Killers, all right. Where are they at?"

"They rode off."

There was no use wasting his time on these breeds. He and Denny could push on and maybe catch Bridges if they had any luck. "Better get your horse. We're going to try to catch that bunch."

"That sounds fine with me." Denny turned on his heel and went to gather his mount.

When he came back leading his and Slocum's horses, he said, "These two got some skinny horses staked down in the draw."

"They can walk. We'll take the horses with us."

"I'll get the packhorse. He's still hobbled."

"Good."

In a short while they were saddled and loaded. Without a word to the two tied-up breeds seated on the ground, they rode off in the night to the southeast, herding the breeds' two horses ahead of them. Slocum wasn't certain of the time. They had only the starlight to guide them, though on the plains that was quite a bit of light. But still, several hours of darkness remained.

Close to sunup, smoke from a cow-chip fire carried on the soft wind.

"Smell it?" Denny asked.

Slocum nodded. They reined up and tried to locate the source. Then they swung their horses south and headed over the next rise. The red glow of the fire showed in the valley below them.

"Reckon that's them?" Denny asked softly.

"Naw, they're too lazy to build a fire this early." Slocum adjusted the Colt on his hip, grateful he'd reloaded it before they set out.

"There's a woman down there." Denny sounded unsure, standing in the stirrups to better see her.

Slocum nodded. "I thought that's what we'd find."

The woman raised up from her cooking, and her startled face shone in the fire's light. In the low illumination, Slocum figured her to be near thirty, with a nice-shaped figure.

"We don't mean you no harm, ma'am," Slocum said as he reined up his horse. "We're just traveling through and saw the light of your fire."

"I'm making some coffee. It'll be ready in a little while. Get down. It's either mighty early or you two are out mighty late." Her gaze followed them as they both nodded and dismounted.

"A little of each." Slocum swept off his hat and his partner did likewise. "Some horse thieves woke us up a few hours ago a bit north of here and we couldn't get back to sleep."

"They must not have gotten your horses."

"No, ma'am. We stopped them. My name is Slocum and this is Denny Kline."

"Ann Looper. Annie is what they call me. My husband, Argus Looper, is supposed to meet me here this morning. I thought I'd make some coffee and biscuits so when he got here we could eat. They're about done—the biscuits anyway."

"We didn't come to impose on you. We're looking for four men who killed Denny's best friend."

"Oh, I'm sorry. You aren't imposing. In fact, I'm glad to see a friendly face after sharing the night out here with the coyotes."

Slocum watched her move, slender-hipped in a divided riding skirt and a long-sleeved white blouse under a feed-sack apron. She was not a short woman, and he liked how she held her long brown hair to one side as she bent over her cooking. For a woman out here alone, she acted confident of herself, so he guessed this was not a role she hadn't experienced before. Nothing brassy about her, but she obviously was not some isolated farmer's wife.

With the hook, she removed the Dutch oven lid and nodded at the sight of her handiwork.

"Here," she said and nimbly took a biscuit out and tossed it to Denny. He shuffled it around from hand to hand—too hot to hold.

Then she did the same to Slocum and laughed. "This ain't you boys' first cow camp."

When the biscuit cooled some, Slocum broke his open and the steam rose out of it. The sourdough smell went straight up his nose and he nodded his approval.

"No butter or jelly, fellows." She finished filling a plate of them.

"This is feast enough for two hungry drifters," Slocum said, chewing on his first bite. "Could I ask why you're out here alone?"

"You can always ask." She smiled at him, setting down the tin plate loaded with biscuits and then taking her place on the buffalo grass close to the two of them. "Argus wants to start a horse ranch right here."

"This is the country you all are going to settle in?" Slocum paused for her answer before reaching for another biscuit.

"That's what we planned. Is there something wrong about that?"

"I don't know, but I'd settle closer to people if I was going to raise and sell horses." *Each to their own choices*, Slocum thought and reached for another biscuit.

"My husband has some grand plans, and he wants lots of land for this operation."

"He sure can find it out here. Which way did you come

up here?" Slocum looked at her in the growing light of dawn.

"I bought three horses in Dodge, oh, four days ago. Two horses for packing 'cause I couldn't lift those big panniers and needed to travel light."

Slocum narrowed his eyes in disbelief at her statement. "You came up here all by yourself?"

"Why, yes."

He shook his head, wondering how her husband could do that to her. "You know, there're still some hostile Indians scattered across this end of Kansas."

She nodded serious-like at his words. "A lieutenant with a small company of soldiers told me that yesterday morning when I was coming up here."

"He told you right."

"I can handle myself."

"The four killers we're looking for also assaulted a rancher's widow up in Nebraska."

"My goodness. I worry more about rattlesnakes and wolves than that happening."

"When is your husband due to get here?"

"Any day now. He said the fifteenth. By my count that's today. Why?"

"'Cause I'm going to leave Denny here to see that nothing happens to you until he arrives."

"Oh, I can't be that big a bother to you two."

"I'd rather be safe than sorry." Denny agreed with Slocum and nodded his approval. Especially with the kinds of men they were dealing with.

"Argus will be coming." She shrugged her shoulders. "That's the least of my concerns."

"It won't hurt for Denny to stay with you until then. You didn't pass four men yesterday, did you?" If she had she might not be here.

"No, I saw those soldiers in the morning and nary a soul after that."

Slocum had one more question for her. "Why didn't your husband meet you in Dodge?"

"Oh, he took a train west from Omaha on business, and he sent me to Dodge City. And I simply rode up here to meet him."

Slocum looked around. "Whatever possessed him to choose this place?"

"The big spring that flows southeast out of here. There's good water down that creek for miles. It starts about a hundred yards south of here."

That was the only thing about her deal that made any sense at all to him. A good flowing spring would be reason enough to settle here. Still, sending his wife off by herself on a wild trip like this was not what he'd call thoughtful behavior by her husband.

He still planned to leave Denny there with her. The sunlight opening up only made him want to ride on and find those four rapists.

"How about some bacon and fried potatoes?" she asked.

"Sure. What can we do to help?"

"Find some more chips for the fire."

"We can do that." Getting up and brushing off their seats, Slocum and Denny nodded at each other and went looking for fuel.

In an hour, Slocum unloaded Denny's bedroll and—despite her protests that she'd be fine alone—he left the young man with her, telling Denny to catch up with him when her man arrived.

"You be careful," Denny said, tightening the packsaddle girths.

"You do the same. After the husband gets here, you try to meet me in Dodge. I have some reason to believe that Bridges's bunch won't stick around Dodge. They'll go on down to Fort Supply for some reason or the other."

"You going to leave me word in Dodge where you went to?"

"Yes. Beaver's Mercantile Store. I'll leave you a letter there if I have to ride on. Be on your toes with her. Anything can happen out here."

"I will, Slocum. I will."

If Barr had ever felt any worse, after the jolting ride back to the ranch in the buckboard with Mozelle handling the reins, he couldn't recall it. The woman was crazy. Sliding corners and about tipping the damn thing over several times. He knew her well enough to realize that she was mad about the abortion. When he asked about Erma, she coldly said that Erma was okay.

When he got back to the ranch, he turned down her offer of food, took some more laudanum and went to bed. Where was Doss anyway? He ignored Erma, who was resting and looked pale.

11

Slocum rode off, leaving Denny with Mrs. Looper and on the lookout for her husband. He wondered whether he was right in believing that Bridges was on the trail ahead of him as he headed southeast. The fact that Annie Looper hadn't seen Bridges and his men though she'd come from that direction bothered him. Of course, she could have been over a ridge and out of sight of the outlaws. There was something strange about a man sending his wife out to nowhere and him not being there to meet her. The whole idea bothered him.

Midday, he spotted a low-walled soddy and some corrals. He rode over and approached the open front door. No dogs barked—only some dusty brown hens and a Shanghai rooster were scratching in the horse apples for some undigested grain.

"Hello, the house."

Nothing.

He approached the half-open door made out of weathered gray wagon flooring. Why was it standing open? A quick look around and he stuck his head inside. "Anyone home?"

He saw a boot. The boot was attached to the leg of someone lying still, facedown on the floor. The sight made him reach for his six-gun. Then he heard someone's choked-up whimpering coming from somewhere farther inside the room.

"I'm a friend," he said, anxious to know if the unseen person might be armed and dangerous.

"Go away. . . ." More sobs.

"I can't. You must need help." Slow-like, he eased the door fully open, letting more light inside. The person, who he suspected was a woman crying, had to be beyond the tousled bed and low enough down that he couldn't see her. He stepped over the still man on the floor. The victim was shot in the back. His blood had already turned dark on his shirt where the powder-burned bullet holes were. Two—no, three bullets.

With fear-filled eyes, the woman on the floor clutched a flannel blanket to hide her nakedness. He swept a quilt off the bed and put it over her shoulders. "I'll go outside while you dress. Call me when you've got your clothes on."

She sobbed.

He gazed at the dead man and then stepped over him. Outside he looked over her ranch. Not a prosperous place, but a homestead chiseled out of the rolling grassland. Two people working hard by themselves in the vastness of the frontier. One was dead; the other one had no doubt been ruthlessly raped by cruel men without any respect for any-one.

He heard a sniff behind his back. He turned and saw her wet eyes. "Who did this to you?"

"Four . . . men."

"You hear their names?"

"B-Bridges—" She moved toward him, all choked up.

He nodded that he understood and hugged her. Rocking her gently, he put her age as in the early twenties and much the junior to the dead man on the floor. A willowy figure in his arms, she was five-foot-six or seven inches tall. Her light brown hair, collar length, was mussed and needed brushing.

"Why did they come here?" she asked.

"I don't know. What do they call you?"

"Meagen—Meagen Holt."

"My name is Slocum."

"Poor Carl—they killed him."

"I can see that." He looked over her head, staring at the neatly cut blocks of sod used to build the house.

She went back to sobbing on him.

"How long ago were they here?"

"They left after dawn. I don't know when—"

"You know we'll have to bury him?"

"Yes. . . ."

"Do you have a shovel?"

"There's one in the barn."

"I'll go find it. You make us some coffee and food. It will take me a couple of hours to dig his grave."

Numb-like, she nodded. "I'll do that. Oh, thanks—"

With a nod to her, he went to unsaddle Buck and his packhorse. With the beasts hobbled and grazing, he headed for the barn. What niggled at him the most was the realization that he had been so close to those killers. Perhaps less than six hours separated them. But for the moment, he'd need to take the time to help Meagen Holt put away her husband. The gang must be headed toward Dodge City. His biggest hope was that the former railhead would stall them long enough for him to catch up with them.

He found the long-handled shovel near the door of the barn. The tool looked to be in good condition. Inside the small barn sat a nearly new Oliver mowing machine, and the barn was full of rich-smelling hay. A rusty red–colored team of draft mares stood in the corral and nickered at him. Obviously Carl had been a hardworking, neat farmer. Armed with the shovel on his shoulder, he went back to the house.

From the doorway, he saw that Meagen had removed her husband's boots and laid him on his back. Slocum bent over and closed the man's eyelids, a thing she probably could not handle.

"You need to show me a place to dig."

"I-I've been thinking. On the rise. He liked to go up there and survey his land."

He tossed his head to the north and she agreed. Then softly he said, "I'll go do it."

"When the food is ready I'll call you."

"That's fine."

"Slocum—my sister and her husband live near Dodge. Maybe I should go there."

He nodded. "We'll have time to figure that out."

The thick sod was the hardest part to cut and lay aside. The ground crumbled as he drove the blade in to the hilt with the arch of his boot and the hole began to take shape. He was near knee-deep when she came up with a cup of coffee for him.

"No cream. Our cow died." She handed it to him. "He was going to buy a new one."

"Thanks. I don't need cream."

"Good. You should come to the house. The bread will be done soon."

"That's not hard to do," he said, scrambling out. Recovering his coffee, he realized they were on a high point and he could imagine her husband coming up here to survey his fiefdom. The mowed acreage looked like it had been given a haircut. They'd done lots of work establishing this place.

Close to sundown, Carl Holt's corpse was wrapped in a blanket, packed up the hill on a sled pulled by one of the Belgian mares and laid to rest in his grave. Slocum said some words of grace and delivered him to his maker.

Then he filled the grave back in, and they went to the house when the stars came out. The plans were that the next morning, he'd take her to her sister's using the team and wagon, and then he'd get on searching for the killers.

Barr woke in the worst mood. Light-headed, he tried to separate things out in his mind. In the kitchen, he collapsed on a ladder-back chair. Mozelle served him coffee.

"Is she all right?" his housekeeper asked.

"She's asleep. How should I know?" He shrugged away any concern for Erma. In his case he had bigger fish to fry.

Mozelle shook her head in disgust and went back to turning the flapjacks that she was stacking up for the ranch hands. "You can go ring the bell for me."

He could smell ham cooking. The smoky flavor in his nose, he went out on the porch and rang the bell. Where was Doss at anyway? He should be coming back with Barr's money. Disgusted, Barr went back inside again to feed his face.

After taking only a few bites, he realized that there was no way he could eat his full breakfast—the pounding headache had returned. He took some laudanum, went into the great room and fell into a stuffed chair until he dozed off.

The men went by him silently enough that he never heard them leave the house. He awoke in a few hours and shouted at the women. "Where did they go?"

Mozelle came to the kitchen door and looked sternly at him. "They went to work, of course."

"I never—"

"You were sound asleep."

"You should have woke me."

"Ha," she said. "And get bit by you."

"I have to go find Doss."

She looked him up and down in disgust. "And fall off your horse out there?"

"Pack some supplies and bedroll in a buckboard. Erma can drive me."

"She could never pick you up if you fall down."

"Never mind. Just get it ready."

He put off leaving until that afternoon, hoping his head would clear up some more. They finally left for town. Halfway there he became sick to his stomach and made her stop so he could barf up everything inside him. Holding on to the iron seat bar he hung over the side, gagging with the dry heaves. The pungent sourness burned his nostrils and eyes until they ran with water.

Using a small towel Erma handed him, he wiped his mouth and blotted his eyes. Then he ordered her to take him on to town and a hotel room—he was too sick to continue his business. When they got to town, he was barely able to climb the stairs to the room, and he quickly passed out across the bed.

When he awoke, it was dark outside and he found Erma asleep on the floor in a bedroll. He stumbled out of the room and went to look for someone he could hire to take with him. After searching in two saloons, he found two unemployed Texans that Doss had told him about, Max Goodall and Maynard Kittles.

He hired the pair to meet him at the livery the following morning to go after the robbers. Then with too much liquor in his empty gut, he staggered back to the hotel room. Once inside he took off his pants and crawled in the bedroll with Erma. But he was too drunk to get up an erection and finally passed out trying.

"Get up. Get up," Erma was urging him. "You told me last night you have to meet the men."

"Yeah." He sat up on the floor, wondering if he had screwed her the night before. He couldn't recall. After she straightened up his clothing and brushed his hair, they left the hotel. On Main Street, they found a café and had some breakfast. He ate sugared oatmeal, hoping it might stay down. One thing he knew, if he couldn't eat he'd eventually become too weak to even ride on the buckboard seat.

At the stables, Goodall told Barr that he'd heard Doss

and his men had been through Wilbur's place, the trading post south of North Platte, a few days before looking for the outlaws. He'd talked to some drifting cowboy he knew who'd come in the night before from down there.

"You sure of that?" Barr asked.

"Pretty reliable word on it."

"Good, we'll go there first. You hear anything about a guy named Slocum?"

Goodall shook his head. "But I know a man here in town who knows a lot. I'll go find him and ask."

While Goodall and Kittles went to look for the man, Barr and Erma waited in the hotel room. Hours later Goodall and Kittles came back empty-handed, and the impatient Barr decided to leave without talking to the informer.

Since Barr was in no condition to ride for long on the seat, Erma made him a pallet in the back of the buckboard and she drove easy. The two cowboys jogged ahead to see what they could learn. It was sundown when Barr and Erma arrived at the trading post. Goodall reported to him that all three groups had passed through there. "Bridges and his men first and a couple days later a guy the barkeep called Slocum and some boy who was riding with him. Then Doss and two men came after that."

"Who was the boy with Slocum?" Barr asked with his butt up against the wheel for support, unable to imagine who it could be. Still not clearheaded, he fought to regain his senses. The headache was back, and that didn't help.

"Don't know. Your man Doss and two others came a day later. Sounds like they're all heading for Dodge."

"We better get there too." Barr shook his sore head. That damn Bridges would pay for his discomfort—damn him anyway.

12

The lights of the onetime queen of the cow towns sparkled in the night before them on the prairie when Slocum reined up Meagen Holt's team of mares. He carried lots of memories about the former railhead on the Arkansas River. But with Kansas shut off by the tick fever quarantine, a legend died, and the town had been taken over by sodbusters.

God-fearing folks replaced all the heyday gamblers, con men, cattle buyers, drovers, wanted outlaws and the damndest supply of shady ladies the West had ever known.

"We can camp down by the river in the bottoms," Slocum said.

Meagen agreed with a nod. "I haven't been here in two years. Carl brought me down here with him to get the new mowing machine."

"I saw it in the barn."

"Oh, it's a good one."

He agreed. "It's been that long or longer since I've been here."

"Do you think the gang'll still be here?"

"I'm not certain. The town's a lot tamer than it used to be. It may not suit them."

She agreed. "Must have been pretty wild in those days?"

"In those days it was wild." He laughed and slapped the mares with the lines to make them keep jogging, towing the wagon, with Slocum's horses tied to the back. It wouldn't be long till they got to the town.

With Meagen set up in the camp, Slocum chewed on some jerky, figuring by the half-moon's travel across the sky that it was close to midnight. Not a time for farmers to be up, but people like Bridges had no alarm clock. He tucked Meagen in her bedroll and then rode Buck into Dodge. Close to town, he wound up his gun belt and stored it in his saddlebags. He knew from past visits about the strict gun rules in Dodge.

Under the coal oil lamp, he found a familiar face in the town marshal's office. With his long legs and dusty boots planted on the desktop, Deputy Marshal Ernie Copland blinked at him.

"Why, Slocum. What in God's green earth brings you back here?" He dropped his boots to the floor and stuck out his hand. "You're a real sight to see."

"Business. Four men arrived in town maybe a day or two ago. Texas drovers, one's a big, tall guy named Bridges. You seen them?"

Copland nodded. "They were here."

"They're gone?" Slocum felt a sharp pain of disappointment.

"I can't say for sure, but I ain't seen them in a day. Dodge ain't much of a place to entertain yourself anymore like it was before."

"I understand. Who'd know where they went?"

"Like always, a bartender. They're the best source I can think of." Copland reached for his hat. "Let's go talk to a few."

"I thought they closed all the Kansas saloons."

"It'll happen soon enough. We've been simply ignoring the order. Since we lost the cattle shipments, folks have hurt bad around here."

Slocum agreed and they headed down Front Street. In the third empty saloon that they tried, they talked to a bartender that Copland called Ed.

"Yeah, they were in here two nights ago. I wondered about the four of them. Where in hell did they get all that money they spent?"

"They cleaned out a rancher's safe in Nebraska," Slocum said.

"Sounds about right. They spoke once about Fort Supply. Of course, it's across the line down in the Indian Territory."

"They mention any reason why they wanted to go there?" Slocum asked.

Ed shook his head. "There ain't much going on down there either."

Slocum thanked him, and he and Copland walked back to the jail.

"What else can I do for you?" Copland asked. "I ain't never forgot you backing me that night in the Wild Horse."

"Hey, that wasn't nothing." Slocum shrugged his shoulders. "I better get back to my camp."

"You get time, come by and see me. I'd like to hear what all you've been up to."

Slocum shrugged again. "I'd love to, but I need to try and catch those four."

"I savvy that. Come by anytime."

Slocum agreed, left the office and rode back to camp. He'd need to leave Denny a note at Beaver's Mercantile in the morning. It was getting on, must be near two o'clock or later. He dropped heavy from the saddle and went to stripping out his latigos. Then he felt someone hugging him from behind, and he twisted around.

"I'm glad you're back. I was scared being out here

alone." Meagen held him in a tight embrace, wearing a thin night sleeping dress.

"Anyone bother you?"

"No, no. I was just afraid, being in a strange place alone, I guess."

"Let me unsaddle him, and I'll be right with you."

"Sure." She released him.

Slocum got the saddle off and hitched Buck so he could eat some of the hay they'd brought for the horses. He turned and Meagen hugged him from the front.

He bent over and kissed her. Her arms locked around his neck, and he swept her up in his arms.

"I'm sorry, Slocum," she said and buried her face in his neck. "I needed someone real bad tonight. Someone to hold and love me—I'm crazy maybe. I just needed you real bad. I ain't imposing, am I?"

"I'm flattered," he said, setting her down on the bedroll.

"Wonderful," she said and began unbuttoning her dress down the front.

He went to toeing off his boots. In a few minutes they were both naked and under the covers against the cool night wind. She was thin, but her boobs were topped with large, rock-hard nipples, and her belly was tight with muscles that she must have earned pitching hay beside her man. Their hungry mouths sought each other, and soon they were lost in the arms of passion.

His middle finger, sliding over her belly, soon found her rising clit. She raised her butt up to his teasing, and she began breathing faster and faster. Then she gasped. "Take me—please. . . ."

He moved on top of her, bracing himself, and she guided the nose of his dick in her gates with her small hand. When he began to enter her with his throbbing hard erection, she threw her head back and groaned as he passed through her tight ring.

"That hurt you?" He frowned down at her, wondering what her problem could be.

"No . . . it's wonderful."

Good. He proceeded to wear a new one in her. She soon clung to him. With her fingernails digging into his back, they rode their bobsled ride to new heights and then soared down the course time and again. She tossed and twisted her head as if she was in ecstasy's arms and was flying with wings.

Then her internal muscles began to tighten. They soon gripped his aching, skintight erection so his brain spun, and then needles in his testicles warned him they soon would crash. He reached beneath her and grasped the half-moons of her tight butt and buried himself inside of her up to her pelvic bone—then he came hard and she cried out, "Yes!"

They sprawled in each other's arms, exhausted and half-way doped by the adrenaline rush. Then her hand grasped his rod and she managed, "He's still alive."

"Barely," Slocum mumbled in her ear and rolled her toward him. In seconds he found her on top of his belly and inserting his half-hard dick inside her slick pussy. His callused hand molded the halves of her small heinie as she bounced up and down on him, waking up his sleeping dick to full power. They finished off that session with him on top, and again his aching balls filled her with another fountain of cum.

They slept with her draped halfway over the top of him until the sun was well up. Then she woke him and scrambled to get up and dress, acting worried that someone would see her naked. Seated on his butt, he chuckled about her concern, pulling on his pants, and she shoved him over with a frown.

After a late breakfast, he asked her if she needed anything from town, and she listed coffee as the most important thing she lacked. He promised to get her some and saddled Buck for the ride in. His main purpose for going back into town was to gather information; he hoped to get more news about Bridges's destination.

He gave her a kiss on the cheek, and she slapped her hand on the spot as if to hold it. Then she shook her head. "You know you're different than any man I've ever known. You're just plumb full of surprises. I can't recall anyone ever kissing me goodbye before in my entire life."

He winked at her. "Well, I'll see ya."

"I'll sure be here, big man."

He rode off for Dodge. In town he spoke to several of the liverymen and blacksmiths. None of them recalled anything about Bridges or his gang. A while later in the Elephant saloon, playing poker with two men, Slocum heard a man ask the bartender if he knew a guy named Bridges. When Slocum turned his ear that way, he learned the man's name was Doss. Who was Doss? If Denny was there he'd probably know the man, but obviously this drover was someone looking for his man too.

The gambler named Donovan nodded, ready to deal, when he said to Doss, "I could help you, stranger. He left two days ago for Fort Supply."

"Were there four of them?"

"Yeah, they were all riding together."

Doss nodded. "Thanks, I better mosey along. Hoped that I'd catch him here."

"What's your business?" Slocum asked, looking at his new cards.

"Bridges robbed my boss. Beat him up badly."

Slocum nodded, like he now knew all he wanted. After Doss left, he tossed in his pasteboards and went to the front window to watch Doss and two others ride off on Barr branded horses. He knew neither of the other two men. One was tall, the other skinny. But if they were that close to Bridges, they might beat him to the punch.

Satisfied he needed to be on the move, he told the gambler he needed to see about some business and left the saloon. He soon learned Doss and the other two had stabled their horses at Kesler's Stables. If Barr had known that Bridges had stolen the money, then they probably hadn't been wearing masks when they stole it. And the multiple rape of Minnie Farley by Bridges and his gang might have been planned by Barr, and the deal had somehow gone sour. Probably Bridges got greedy and took all of Barr's money. This development answered lots of questions for Slocum.

If only he knew why Fort Supply was on Bridges's list of places to go next. There was something at that outpost that involved Bridges, and Slocum might not be able to wait on Denny to get to Dodge. Best he could do was leave a note at the store for Denny. Slocum headed over to Beaver's Mercantile and left Denny a letter telling the young man to come on to Fort Supply as soon as he could. He also left a few dollars in the envelope in case the boy needed some money.

Next he bought Meagen the coffee and some candy, then headed back to camp. When he got there, she had on overalls, her hair was braided and she was wearing a cowboy hat.

"You're all dressed up to work," he said, handing her the candy and the coffee in the poke.

"Well, my, my. Lemon drops." She popped one in her mouth and grinned big. Moving it around with her tongue, she said, "I've been thinking you can use a cook while you're looking for those men. I want to take my team and wagon over to my sister's, borrow a saddle horse from them and go with you. I want those bastards caught as bad as anyone."

"Meagen—"

She ran over and silenced him with her finger on his mouth. "I can also do other things to earn my keep besides cook."

"These men are dangerous—"

"I know damn good and well. I was the point of their horny wrath."

"But—"

"I'm going along with you or I'll follow you. What will it be?"

"Lunch, I guess."

She jumped up and down, then threw her arms around his neck and gave him a lemony sweet kiss.

With the team boarded and the wagon parked at her sister's house and a saddle horse borrowed, they acted like they had to leave in a hurry. Despite Meagen's sister wanting her to stay overnight, they rode on.

Meagen looked back to be certain they were out of hearing. "Guess she figured out why we were in a hurry to leave."

"Oh?" Slocum said, acting dumb.

"Damn you." She rode in close and gave him a playful shove. "You're addictive."

"I been called lots of things, but never that."

"You are anyway. Where are we camping?"

"Across the river."

"Good, we can take a nap."

"Ah, sleep some," he said.

"You can do that anytime. I've got bigger plans. Much bigger ones than that." Then she laughed and pushed her cowboy hat back on her shoulders. The cord caught on her throat. "Oh, yes."

What had he unleashed in this woman? My, my!

With the help of some laudanum, Barr slept in the back of the buckboard most of two days to escape his acute headache. Erma drove the rig hard, and his two hired hands rode ahead to learn all they could about Slocum's, Doss's and Bridges's travels.

When Barr awoke, they had stopped. Goodall was talking to a woman—some well-dressed lady he hadn't expected to find out there. Barr half raised himself. Sitting up at last, he asked Erma, who had dismounted from the buck-board, who his man was visiting with over there.

"A Mrs. Looper," Erma said under her breath.

"What's she doing out here alone?"

"I don't think she's alone. There's a young man with her."

"What's his name?"

Erma shook her head. "I ain't heard. But he sure ain't her husband—he's too young to be that."

Barr cut a hard look at her, "He around here?"

"No, I only seen him when we first stopped."

"You recognize him?"

She shook her head.

Goodall came back over and spoke in a low voice to Barr. "She says Slocum was through here a few days ago. But she ain't never seen Bridges nor Doss."

"Where did Slocum go?"

"To Dodge. That boy is supposed to catch up with Slo-cum whenever her husband arrives."

"When will her husband be back here?"

"I'd say he was overdue now."

"Hmm." Barr tried to put it all together. "If Slocum had come by here, why hadn't Doss? It don't make sense."

"She never saw Bridges either. But she knows about him because of Slocum stopping off and leaving that boy to help her."

"If Slocum don't have a posse, we might simply elimi-nate him when we catch him. That sumbitch is a trouble-maker." If they even knew what he looked like—something they'd have to figure out too.

"Whatever you say, boss."

"We'll see when we run him down."

"You want to camp here?" Erma asked Barr.

"No." He gave a head toss at the woman. "The less these two know about our business the better."

Erma climbed back on the seat with a scowl and undid

the lines. Then she clucked to the team and drove on, leaving dust in her wake. Barr's men stood in the stirrups and galloped past her.

"You ever see that boy he left with her?" Barr called out to them.

"I didn't know him." Goodall reined up short and shook his head.

"I just wondered why Slocum left the boy."

Goodall shrugged his shoulders. "How would I know that?"

"Never mind." Barr lay back on the pillow. His man was no help. Oh, how would he ever shake all this headache business? The buckboard jolted him hard. Damn, this bucking ride was hard on him too.

13

In the morning, Slocum and Meagen rode south, leading the packhorse. They learned from a freighter they met on their way in the afternoon that Bridges and the others were a good two days ahead of them. But Slocum didn't worry about the distance, and they trotted down the well established road that led to the Indian Territory and Fort Supply.

That night he and Meagen camped well off the road near a small stream. He gathered enough dry wood and sticks that she had plenty of fuel to cook supper over a wood fire instead of using cow chips. His efforts pleased her, and she soon had coffee brewing on the flames.

"Will you know Bridges when we meet him?" he asked her.

"I won't forget that conceited bastard's face for anything."

"I'm sorry to bring the subject up, but I've never met him."

She nodded. "He's as tall as you are. Thinks he's ladies' man." She wrinkled her nose. "He's really not. Wears a handlebar mustache with some gray in it."

He could read the hatred seething behind her eyes. Then she swung her attention back to the sizzling bacon and turned it. "I want to kill him."

"Don't let your anger overload you," he said. "We'll catch him."

"Yes, but every hour he breathes in this world is an hour too long for me."

Slocum understood the fire in her intentions. The same kind of anger drove him on this long chase—what they'd done to Charley's wife, Minnie, stung him deep inside. Perhaps because he'd arrived too late to save his old friend's life, the whole matter made his stomach upset whenever he reflected on all that had happened.

Short of the Indian Territory line later the next afternoon, they found a trading post. Slocum wanted to check it out, so he left Meagen with the horses and crossed the road. The door to the low-walled adobe building was covered with a well-worn buffalo hide. He pulled the hide aside and ducked past it.

In the dim candlelit room, he discovered a bearded man standing behind a counter made of planks on barrels. The place stunk of the body odors of many unwashed customers and the horse shit they'd tracked inside on their boots.

"Welcome to Hell." the man said.

"You the devil?" Slocum asked, amused.

He shook his head and smiled. "Young's my name."

"Slocum's mine. I'm looking for four men who came through here in the last few days."

"What's your business with them?"

"They murdered some men and raped some good women. The leader was called Bridges."

"Big guy with a mustache?"

"That's the leader."

"They ain't here. Rode on, I guess. They stopped by and bought a few pints of cough medicine."

Slocum nodded. He knew that most of Kansas had joined

the prohibition business, and what this man called "cough medicine" was really whiskey in a pint bottle that could be stuffed in your boot—a practice that eventually led to the term "bootlegger." The Indian Territory's borders, patrolled by deputy U.S. marshals out of Fort Smith, had been dry for years, and so liquor in that land was not only scarce but commanded a higher price.

"When were they here?" Slocum asked.

"Yesterday, I reckon. You have a posse?"

Slocum shook his head.

The man frowned at his reply. "They looked pretty tough for one man to buck up against."

"I appreciate your concern." He thought about buying a bottle of "cough medicine," but passed on the matter, paying the man two dollars for his information and leaving.

"What did you find out?" Meagen asked, holding out his reins for him.

"They were here yesterday."

Stone-faced, she nodded. "We're close to them, then?"

"I think so." In the saddle, he twisted around, looking back up the road, wondering where that boy was at. Surely by this time Mrs. Looper's husband had shown up. But Slocum saw nothing. They rode on.

In the late afternoon, they found a moon lake with cattails growing around the edge. Several ducks burst out of the water and took wing.

"How deep do you think that water is?" Meagen asked.

"Maybe knee-deep out there a good ways." Most playas like this weren't much deeper than that, though this one might be.

"I don't care. I need a bath if you don't mind."

He took off his hat and wiped his sweaty brow on his shirtsleeve. "That won't hurt. We'll hobble the horses. I've got soap and one towel."

"Sounds delightful. You can scrub my back."

"Sure." He'd been so involved in his pursuit of the

outlaws, the notion of her as woman hadn't been something he'd thought about. For the first time in two days, he began to consider her as a woman rather than as simply his companion—slender and willowy, she wasn't hard to look at, not at all.

After hobbling the horses, he fetched the soap and two towels out of his saddlebags. She shook her head at the sight of the two towels. "You said you only had one."

"I lie—sometimes."

She ran over and hugged him. With a flip of her head, she tossed her light brown hair back. "What happens out here is between you and me?"

"Sure."

With his reply, she squeezed his face between her palms and kissed him—hard. He dropped the towels and soap in the grass, then gathered her lithe figure in his arms. Her tongue was hot and challenging. What an awakening he'd discovered.

Out of breath, she buried her face in his chest. "I lay awake last night, wanting to crawl into your arms again. I sure needed you to hold me again."

"Why didn't you wake me? Life's too short not to enjoy every passing hour."

"I was afraid that you hadn't enjoyed me the night before or that I might appear too demanding."

He lowered his forehead to the top of her head. "I really enjoyed you. I hope you can enjoy it again."

"I will, Slocum. I promise you I will."

They began to undress in the bloody sundown's glow. In minutes she was naked, wading out into the lake ahead of him. Her small, shapely rump brought a smile to his windsore face.

She turned in the knee-deep water, and her pear-shaped breasts looked like they were capped by pointed stars. "This must be as deep as the water gets."

He hurried out, caught her, turned her toward him and

then kissed her hard on the mouth. "It's good enough for me."

Her body lathered up, she looked like a snow princess to him as he tossed handfuls of water on her to rinse away the residue. When she was at last free of the suds, she set in to scrubbing him, and her small hands on his skin stirred him. With the soap at last rinsed away, he swept her up in his arms and waded to shore. He set her down near their horses and ran to untie a bedroll. *Why did everything take so long when you were in a hurry?*

At last he rolled the ground cloth out, and they dropped to their knees on it with their lips locked. Soon she scrambled underneath him and reached beneath his belly to clench her fist around his erection. The nose of his dick poised at her gates, he eased himself inside, up to her restrictive ring. She raised her butt off the bedroll and closed her eyes for his swift entry, clutching his arms until he thrust his full length all the way into her.

Her moans made him glance down, worried about causing her pain. But the slow grin on her face convinced him— she wanted no holds barred. He gave her all he had, and she arched her back for more. Her small heels pounding his calves, he flew into a fury on top of her.

Underneath him, she tossed her head from side to side, lost in passion's wildfire. Soon he felt a tingling in the bottom of his scrotum. He drove his bullet deep inside and fired his gun—she half fainted and then came back groggy.

"Oh, my God. . . ." She clung to him. "Don't leave me yet."

So he stayed on top of her for yet another round. Totally spent after that second go-round, they fell asleep without any supper.

Sometime later he awoke, and careful not to rouse her, he eased out from beneath the covers. Under the stars he got up, and with the cooler night air sweeping his bare skin, he went to check on the horse stock. He unloaded them and went back on his tender soles to the bedroll. He swept his feet off and crawled in against her warm form. She reached back, patted his leg, then let her hand rest there. The warmth of her soft touch followed him back into sleep.

Barr barely made it from the wagon to his bedroll. Erma half supported him and, in the dying sunset, helped him ease down on his pallet.

"We've been riding so hard after these men," she whispered. "You need to rest for a day or so and get your strength back."

"Easy for you to say," he grumbled. "Those bastards have all my money."

"Hmm," she snuffed through her nose. "And if you caught these robbers, then what could you do to them?"

"I could kill them. I guarantee you I could. Now hush up. Here comes the help."

"You know this man Slocum is only a short distance ahead of us?" Goodall said, coming up to squat in front of Barr.

"You find his camp?"

"No, but the last freighter I talked to said that he saw him only a day ahead. I just wondered what you wanted to do about him."

"Kill the son of a bitch. He ain't of any value to me."

"There's a woman riding with him," Goodall said.

"She could be a witness against us."

Goodall shook his head. "I just wondered if you had any interest in her."

Barr shook his head. "Handle it."

"We can do that."

"Oh, and be careful. He ain't no dumb hick farmer. A man hired him or was going to hire him as a gun hand."

"Only takes one bullet." Then Goodall, with his buddy Kittles, went to collect some more cow chips for Erma's cooking fire.

"I thought you were going to use Slocum to get Bridges for you?" Erma asked in a whisper after the men left.

"This whole damn thing has gone on too long. They'll have all my money spent before I get them at this rate. Better to eliminate him. One less problem."

"What about your foreman Doss?"

"What about him? He couldn't find his ass. He's ahead of Slocum somewhere, I guess."

"All this confuses me." She shook her head.

"Me too." He lay back down and closed his eyes. The damn pounding headache was driving him nuts.

After taking a big dose of laudanum, he finally fell into a restless sleep.

14

The next morning passed uneventfully. Slocum and Meagen made slow time as he stayed busy reading the tracks—one of Bridges's bunch rode a horse with crooked front legs, and Slocum watched for its hoofprints.

They were stopped on a shallow stream that wandered around sand piles, watering their horses under some cottonwoods. The small leaves rattled in the south wind. A bullet whined through the grove, and Slocum jerked the rifle out of his scabbard, shouting for Meagen to get down.

Who in hell was shooting at them? He saw another puff of smoke, and the incoming round threw chips of cottonwood bark all over him. Then the report came across the rolling country.

"I see someone on that ridge," Meagen said, lying on her belly behind a rotting log.

"There's more than one out there. They're picking their shots. I figure that must be his foreman. Name's Doss."

"Why in the hell are they shooting at us?" She frowned, displeased.

"No telling," he said, taking aim above the small figure

on the ridge. He'd need lots of trajectory to even send a bullet that far and would be less than accurate. His finger squeezed off the shot, and he let the acrid gun smoke be swept away from his gun barrel.

The bullet drew a puff of dust close by his target. That was all for that one; the ambusher got up and ran out of sight to the north.

She laughed. "He damn sure hightailed it. Why, I'd bet he never expected for you to get that close to him with hot lead."

"Probably didn't." He watched the edge of the ridge they were on for any more signs of activity.

"I'll go get the horses and keep them out of sight." She scrambled to her feet and, running bent over, hurried off. The ponies weren't far, and she had the right idea.

"Keep your head down." He seriously studied the surrounding rises.

Then he saw a rider and two packhorses headed toward them. Another person on horseback was tailing them and quirting the packhorses to make them go faster. Slocum squinted, trying to see who it was.

"Who is it that's coming?" Out of breath, Meagen joined him.

"The boy Denny and Mrs. Looper, I think."

"Where's her husband?" Meagen asked, still gasping, and dropped in beside him. "Wasn't she going to meet her man up there?"

Slocum shook his head over the deal, watching for anyone pursuing them. "Damned if I know. But it's them."

"Maybe they'll know the shooters."

"I expect they do and are taking the break to pass them."

The four horses were coming hard. The sound of their hooves beating the ground and their heavy breathing soon came into earshot.

"Whoa," Denny shouted at his mount, skidding him to a stop. "It's them all right, Annie."

Mrs. Looper nodded and swung down. Holding her hips, she bent over to stretch her back. "Whew! We decided to come by them when that one went running back for his horse like his pants were on fire. You two all right?"

"We're fine. Meagen, meet Annie Looper. I wasn't expecting you, but it's good to see both of you."

Denny smiled at her, then dismounted and removed his hat for Meagen. "I got your money in Dodge, Slocum. Ain't spent any of it."

Slocum nodded. "Meagen, this is Denny, my man. Well, tell us what you two know."

"That was Barr's foreman, Doss, and two guys he must have picked up to back him who were shooting at you. I didn't recognize them two. They ain't from his regular Barr Ranch bunch. I know most of them on sight. And back behind them somewhere is Barr. Him and some woman came by Annie's camp up in Kansas with two more strangers, and I stayed out of sight—but I knew they were after Bridges, and I guess they thought you were in their way of getting to him. Barr looked in bad shape, but I only got a glimpse of him. His two riders are new guys too, so they didn't know me. I took a powder from camp when they came in."

Slocum turned and frowned at Mrs. Looper. "Your husband never showed up?"

She shook her head as if embarrassed. "Oh, that's a long story."

"I guess we have time."

"After you left, a Pinkerton man came by my camp looking for him. Said he'd trailed Argus from Omaha and told me about all this counterfeit money he had spent on the way. Lost his tracks near our camp, so I figured that Argus must have doubled back when he realized the agent was after him. So after seven years of marriage, I learned I was married to a counterfeiter."

"What will you do now?" Slocum asked her.

"Divorce him for abandoning me. I have some real money

of my own. I'm going to buy a ranch somewhere out here and settle down. Denny has agreed to be my foreman when we find the right place."

"He's a good man," Slocum said, pleased that the boy had all that figured out. "Now you're here, we need to get after Bridges and capture him. Then, since we have both Doss and Barr behind us, we'll need eyes in the backs of our heads."

Meagen laughed.

"We heard that first shot," Denny said. "And I figured they had you denned up. I told her we could go around them. That's how we caught up."

"We'll either find Bridges, or they'll make a better attempt to plant us. Everyone needs to be aware of what's happening around us. It may get tough."

"We riding on?" Meagen asked.

"We better. Bridges can't be that far ahead."

"Where's he going anyway?" Denny asked.

"Fort Supply is where we think he's headed."

"What's there?"

"Nothing worth wondering about that I know of. It's an old army supply base, and I doubt they even use it anymore."

Slocum looked off to the north and asked Denny, "You see any more of them?"

"Naw, we were over the ridge. Besides, we were traveling fast to circle them."

Satisfied, Slocum nodded his head. "There used to be a small community ahead. We might hole up there for the night in case Barr comes after us." Slocum took Buck's reins from Meagen and swung up in the saddle with a thank-you to her.

He really needed numbers to take on Bridges; an inexperienced boy and two women didn't make for a tough posse. If Barr got both of his bunches together, they'd make too big a crowd for Slocum, Denny and two women to handle.

For the moment, he worried more about Barr's bunch—Bridges knew little about the fact that Slocum was following his crew, and Bridges was simply lighting a shuck to get away.

In the twilight, the dark buildings and old corrals loomed on the prairie. The place appeared to be abandoned. Which one of the structures would be the best one to use as a fort? One where they could hide their horses inside, Slocum decided. They sure didn't need to be afoot out here, forty miles from nowhere.

"I have a spare .30-caliber pistol I can load. It takes black powder as the gunpowder, but doesn't kick like my .44," Slocum offered as the four rode in closer.

"Let me have it," Meagen said.

"I can fire a rifle," Annie said. "But as for hitting someone I'm not sure about, I always closed my eyes when I pulled the trigger."

"This time keep them open. Maybe simply reloading our arms would be enough."

"Sure, I can do that."

"You figure that bunch back there will charge us?" Meagen asked Slocum.

"Damned if I know. They didn't act very brave the last time. I don't want to take a chance on it."

Inside the largest of the buildings, Slocum held up a lighted torpedo match to see the old saloon's interior with the back portion of the sod roof gone. It looked like the best place, and the most defensible. Their horses were put in the back room and left saddled.

All the ammo they owned was out, placed to be handy. Slocum pointed out the positions around the room he wanted everyone to take. Slocum would have liked to have had more ammo, but they would simply need to make what they had count. Seated on their butts, they silently chewed on hard jerky and waited in the dark. When it grew late, Slocum decided that if there were any attackers coming after them, they would wait till daylight. He sent the two women off to sleep for a while in the bedrolls.

Crickets and an occasional coyote broke the dark silence. He slipped outside with the rifle and listened to every creak and small crack in the night. The grunts of the sleeping horses were obvious. He tried to locate any other sound of other horses or invaders trying to slip up on them.

His eyes dilated, he could see fairly well. The shadows were deeper near the buildings, and he tried to stay in the cover. Searching the rolling hills from the edge of the town, he saw nothing out there in the night. No sign that anyone was anywhere near the buildings—so far. In a short while, he eased back into the old saloon.

"You learn anything?" Denny whispered.

"Nothing so far. Get some sleep."

"What about you?"

"I'll be fine."

At dawn, they made a small fire outside and boiled water for coffee. Annie went around and filled everyone's cup.

Denny asked, "You still think they're coming?"

Slocum nodded. "They may need to get up their nerve. These men ain't the bravest I've ever been up against."

"What if they didn't track us here?"

"That would be good." Slocum blew on his steaming coffee. He was ready for a real meal—something besides jerky. But hot coffee would be the best they got for a while.

The day passed, and the women watered the horses under the men's rifle-armed guard. Back inside the saloon, they fed the horses with feed bags hung on their heads.

Slocum scaled the roof, being careful to find firm places to put his feet with each step, and then he surveyed the country. No sign of any potential shooters. What was taking them so long? If their followers weren't there by nightfall, Slocum's group would pull out again. Rifle in his hands, he fretted. These men aimed to kill them. He needed to remember that. Standing, looking across the brown grass waving in the growing wind, he wondered who was the worst of the two: Barr or Bridges.

Groggy and hungover, Barr sat beside Erma on the spring seat. Through his bleary eyes, he kept searching across the grassland. "Damn, how could they have lost Slocum?"

"I don't know," she said, and then she slapped the weary team with the lines. "These horses need some rest."

"The hell with the horses. They can rest when we find Slocum's group. We've got to find them."

She shrugged in surrender and again slapped the team with the lines.

The day wore on, but Barr was convinced that Slocum had lost them. They reined up at a small moon lake.

"No sign of them, boss," Goodall said, dropping heavily from the saddle.

"Where did they go?"

"Hard to track anyone in this grass in the dark. Guess they cut off and went another way."

Filled with anger, Barr fumbled around to get off the buckboard. Out of breath and standing beside the rig, he had to stop and catch his wind. "Now we've lost him. Where in the hell is Bridges?"

"I guess Fort Supply. That's where we heard he was headed."

"Water these horses for Erma, and we'll head for there next."

"What about Slocum?"

"We've lost him. He'll show up." He drew a deep breath. "We'll get that son of a bitch too."

Damn, if he'd only get his strength back. Maybe Erma was right and he should rest—but there was no time for that. No way. He needed what was left of his money.

15

Slocum led the way as his group rode out of the ghost town in the sundown's dying flames. The six horses came in a line, with Denny bringing up the drag. The two packhorses jogged along without much persuasion, each being led by one of the women.

The plans they'd discussed were to head more southeast and either cut back to the main road or head for the old army base on the strong stream that watered it. *Nothing like leading a small army,* Slocum thought.

They were on the main road by midnight, and under the stars they made good time. When they got close enough to Fort Supply, the lights in the distance indicated the small settlement ahead. He didn't want to be discovered, so they went off the road and made a hasty camp. Horses hitched on a strung picket line. Denny took first watch.

Slocum rolled up in a blanket and closed his dry eyes for a short while. In no time, Denny woke him.

"A buckboard went through just now on the road with two riders. I believe it was Barr and his bunch."

"You pretty sure?"

"Yeah. Barr had some girl driving the rig when he came by Mrs. Looper's camp."

"I kinda figured after that guy shot at us that Barr must have joined up with his man Doss."

"I couldn't see real well, but it looked like it was the same two that came by our camp up there. Just two riders, but their horses sounded done in."

"Good."

"What're we going to do?"

"Let everyone get some sleep." Slocum threw back his covers. "You catch a few winks."

"I'm all right."

"Get some sleep. It may get scarce from here on."

"All right. Slocum, I hope you don't think I'm running out on you. But being her foreman sounded pretty swell."

"No. It's a better opportunity than I have for you."

"Hey, we're going with you to Fort Supply."

"I know. Get some sleep."

"Sure."

Slocum took his rifle and climbed up on the rise to keep an eye out. The crickets chirping had slowed with the drop of night's temperature. Seated cross-legged, he tried to put it all together—Barr and his foreman Doss must be meeting somewhere. How could they have left any communication for each other, or even had any? He chewed on his lower lip; the whiskers felt sharp around his mouth.

There had to be an answer. Maybe Slocum had done things by himself for so long, he couldn't push others like he did himself. If he simply left Denny and the two women there and set out, he'd find Bridges and settle his score with him. This business about Barr and his posses was only making it more complicated. Hell, he'd figure it out sooner or later.

Before dawn they were all up and eating some jerky. Slocum had made coffee while they slept, so they washed down the peppery dried beef with his hot brew. Everyone hurried to get their mounts saddled and loaded. In no time, they were in the saddle and headed for Fort Supply. Their horses acted fresh. The grain had helped them.

That could be the difference. He knew a shortcut. When the sun rose, Slocum led them off the main road and crossed Wolf Creek down a steep-sided gorge, following a trail cut by buffalo over the years. The descent down the bank was hard on the horses. Then they scrambled up the far side, slipping on their wet hooves, but they all made it right side up and emerged on the flats.

Slocum nodded his approval when Denny emerged from the crossing and the girls shouted, "Hooray!"

They set off in a long lope through the grass, and when they reined their mounts down to a walk, the military base sat on the flat ahead of them. There was a post-walled teamsters' cottage a hundred yards ahead: the civilian teamsters' stopover.

"You women stay back until we wave you in. That cottage is the most likely place they'd be. Denny, you go right, I'll go left. Have your gun ready."

The youth gave him a grim nod and held the .45 Colt in his right hand. They charged for the building standing alone by itself away from the stockade. Slocum rode in fast, swinging Buck around hard in front and putting the stop on him. He kicked out of the stirrups, slipped off the saddle and hit the ground, pistol cocked and ready.

"Bridges, get out here," Slocum ordered.

Denny stood apart from him, and when the first man rushed out the door, he cleared his throat. Slocum knew it was one of the gang. In his haste to clear the entrance, the gang member fired his first shot in the porch roof, and then he took two bullets in his chest. Slocum reached the porch, standing over the body. "If you don't aim to die, shuck your guns. Then put your hands up and get out here or you're going to die like this guy out here."

"Hold your fire." The voice sounded desperate.

"Any tricks, you die too."

"I'm coming, I'm coming."

A bareheaded man came out, wide-eyed, with his hands in the sky.

"That's Mike," Denny said about the shaking one. "The one on the porch is Lester."

"Where's Bridges?" Slocum asked Mike, shoving him up against the post wall.

The frightened outlaw swallowed hard. "Him—him and Horace run out on us last night."

"You better not be lying to me."

"I swear to God. That sumbitch rode out and left us nothing."

"Why?"

"I don't know. He never left us a dime either."

Slocum narrowed his eyes at his prisoner. "You know where he went?"

"Tascosa."

"Why did he come here in the first place?"

"He said he had an interest here."

"What was that?" Slocum frowned.

"Hell, I don't know. I wish I'd never even known the sumbitch."

"Hell, it wasn't only Mrs. Farley you bastards raped, but another poor farm wife as well, and you murdered her husband."

"What'cha going to do to me?" The outlaw was trembling and, from the dark stain in the crotch of his pants, had no doubt pissed himself.

"What do you think? Hang your worthless ass. Him too if he ain't dead." Slocum holstered his six-gun. The women arrived about then. Reining up, Meagen frowned at the man before him. "That's one of those damn rutting goats."

"His buddies Bridges and Horace have abandoned them, he says."

"Hold your fire," someone shouted from inside. "We ain't no part of this deal."

"Come on out," Slocum said, shoving Mike at Denny. Slocum held his gun ready again while four scruffy teamsters with their hands in the air came outside, as did a storekeeper in a soiled apron. Behind him came a fat whore, who shook her head. "You guys scared the bejesus out of me."

Slocum uncocked his six-gun. "You can put your hands down. Anyone hear where Bridges was going?"

"Didn't hear him say nothing about it," the storekeeper said. "Been here a couple of days, then got them two drunk as hooters last night and skipped out."

"He ever feed his horses anything?"

The storekeeper shrugged.

"Get up fifty pounds of corn," Slocum said to him, then turned to the women. "Those two"—he nodded toward Bridges's men—"have got horses here. Find them. We're not waiting long here."

"They're still saddled," a whiskered teamster said with a head toss toward some pens. "I can get them."

"Fine."

Meagen gave Annie the lead rope to her packhorse. She rode over with the man to hold the gate for him as he went inside so as not to lose any other animal. He soon returned with two thin, still-saddled horses, and after he hooked the gate, he led them back to the cottage.

"You can damn sure see that they weren't in no shape to go far on these hides," the teamster said.

Slocum agreed. He had one noose nearly made and, satisfied, he cut the other end of the rope. "There's a cottonwood tall enough there. Take him down there." He motioned to Denny to do his bidding.

"Want us to load the other?" a teamster asked.

"He's dead," the storekeeper said, kneeled beside him.

"That's a damn shame," Meagen said, turning her lip up in fiery disgust.

The other outlaw was loaded on his horse and the noose secured. He began talking in gibberish, whining about how they ought to forgive him and how he'd never do anything like it again.

"You son of a bitch, you can tell 'em all about it in hell," Meagen said, and she whipped the horse with a lariat on the butt. The prisoner jerked on the end of the noose and danced in midair, but soon slumped into death.

"What now?" Meagen asked, looking close to trembling.

"We go after Bridges."

"Fine."

"Annie, you and Denny can go on if you want to."

"Not if you need us," Annie said.

"No, we can handle it. There's just Bridges and his partner left. They're going to some outlaw den out in West Texas. Two can get around better than four. We'll get them. Thanks to both of you for your help."

"What about Barr and his bunch?" Denny asked.

"He ain't in no shape, sleeping in a rig, letting a woman drive him. But I expect he'll be here any minute."

Denny shook his head as if uncertain. "Still, he's got some hard cases with him."

"I don't think he'll be a problem if you two swing wide of them leaving here."

"We can do that," Annie agreed.

She came over and thanked Slocum with a brief hug. "You two take care of yourselves."

"Been doing that for years."

He shook Denny's hand, and they gave each other a clap on the shoulder for good luck. "Be certain you go wide now."

"We'll do it."

With his packhorse, Slocum and Meagen rode out to the south, leaving Denny and Annie to head north on their way out of Fort Supply. They should avoid both of Barr's bunches that way. He waved at them and then he spurred Buck to catch up with Meagen. The new sack of grain was on the top of the panniers. Good enough.

"Where in the hell did Bridges go now?" Barr demanded. He got off the buckboard with Goodall's help. He stared at the Bridges gang member who swung in the wind on the noose hanging from the cottonwood tree. What had happened? How in the hell had Slocum beat them here? They must have ridden past Slocum out west of town.

Barr and his bunch drove back to the cottage to learn what they could.

A bearded bear of a man in buckskin came out and looked them over, then he spat to the side. "Bridges left last night and left two of his men behind. Then that big fellow and that boy came riding in here like hell was on fire. Gunned down this one's stupid buddy, who came out and shot a hole in the porch roof. Two women joined them, and they strung up this one hanging there in that cotton-wood tree."

"Where did they go?" Barr asked.

"Two rode north and two rode south."

"Who rode south?"

"The big guy and the gal in braids."

"Who was the guy with the other gal?"

"Damned if I know. Tough kid though. He looked as tough as the big guy."

"What the hell are we going to do now?" Goodall asked.

Barr leaned his throbbing forehead on the iron rail that went around the spring seat. Damn, he hurt. Two of Bridges's bunch without any of his money had been shot and hung. Bridges and one other had left the night before and were still a day ahead.

And Bridges must still have some of the money. How much could he have spent in this godforsaken windy country? Damn, this was a pile of bullshit. His shoulders shuddered when he breathed deep.

"Find me a new team," Barr finally managed.

"Here? Why, they'll cost a fortune," Goodall said.

"I don't give a damn."

"You reckon that was that same fancy woman and boy that we talked to a couple of days ago?" Goodall asked.

"If it was, they rode north, I'd bet," Barr said. "I don't care where the hell they went. You take the best horse we have left and run down that damn Slocum. If he gets to Bridges first, he'll get my money and have it all spent if we don't stop him."

"What about a fresh team for you?"

"I'll have Kittles here go find me one. You need to be on Slocum's ass right now. He's got a two-hour head start."

"I'm going," Goodall said. "And I'll get Slocum."

"Get Bridges as well," Barr shouted after him.

"Mr. Barr?" Maynard Kittles, the other cowboy who'd come with them from North Platte, called out. "Where are you getting this here team?"

Barr looked around. Where would he get a good team? He damn sure had little money left. Maybe away from this place he'd find a cheap team—somewhere.

Goodall was riding out. He could see their horses were worn out too. If their horses had been fresh, they'd have been here sooner too. They might have gotten Slocum as well.

"We can make it a ways farther," Barr said to Kittles. "Erma can drive me. You just follow Slocum's tracks. And don't lose them."

"Shucks, Mr. Barr, why, I could track a mouse over a rock. But these horses sure are give out."

"I know, I know. We'll find some." He gave a head toss to Erma for them to get on their way. She came around, holding her hem up, to help him onto the seat.

Once he was loaded, she climbed up and took the lines. Barr could tell she was mad and upset at him. The horses were done in, but he doubted there was even a horse for sale here. At home on the ranch he had plenty of good fresh horses, but they were several hundred miles north of here. No good to him at the moment.

They followed the military road south. Barr grew dizzier by the hour, and the horses stumbled and snorted with their heads in the dust.

He was half-asleep on the spring seat when Kittles brought an Injun up to their stopped wagon.

"Mr. Barr, this here is Two Hawks. He says he has some fresh horses for sale."

Barr blinked his eyes to focus on the old, gray-headed red man with an eagle feather in his braids. "What do you want for two good horses? Make it three horses."

"Plenty gold."

Pained, Barr looked at the wrinkle-faced old man. "I can give you my check for the money."

"No take paper. It can blow away." Two Hawks shook his head.

"But it is perfectly safe."

Two Hawks shook his head.

"How much do you want for them?" Barr asked.

"Mr. Barr," Kittles said as if Barr couldn't understand the blanket-ass Injun. "Two Hawks wants cash money fur them."

"How much you got on you?" Barr asked.

"Me, Mr. Barr?" Wide-eyed, Kittles swallowed hard at the request.

"Yes, I need to borrow it." He held out his hand for it.

"Why—" Kittles stood in the stirrups to dig in his pockets. In a short while, counting almost out loud, he owned up to having seven dollars and twenty-two cents.

"Tell him he can have all your money, my gold watch and our three good horses for three fine ones."

"Shucks, Mr. Barr, what's an ellit-erate Injun going to do with that gold watch?"

"I don't care if he sticks it up his ass. Ask him."

Two Hawks rode up close and Barr dangled the expensive timepiece for him to see it. In disgust, Barr remembered that the watch had cost a hundred fifty dollars.

The Injun took it, put it to his ear to listen and then nodded. "Me go get horses. We make big trade."

"Good. How long will you be?" Barr made "gimme" motions with his fingers for the Injun to give the watch back.

Two Hawks acted satisfied and gave it back to him.

"Mr. Two Hawks, how long 'fore you get back with them new horses that he is buying? Mr. Barr is asking."

"Me catch 'em and come back with 'em."

"Thank you, Mr. Two Hawks. We'll be a-waiting right here—sir." Kittles turned back. "Mr. Barr he says—"

Scowling, Barr watched the Injun ride off. "I heard that sumbitch fine. No hurrying a damn blanket-ass Injun."

No use even trying.

16

At the crossroads, Slocum shook his head, circling around on horseback and looking in the dust for the direction that Bridges and his man had ridden off.

Then with a nod and a head toss at Meagen, they took the left fork. The windswept grass rolled in waves over the hills.

"Where do you call home?" she asked, riding in close and pulling the string tight that held her straw hat on her head.

"Wherever I throw down my bedroll."

Blinking her blue eyes at his reply, she shook her head in disbelief. "I can't imagine you don't have any more roots than that."

"It's a long story. Someday when we get time I'll tell you all about it."

"I'd love to hear it."

He shrugged. "It ain't all that great."

"Where is this Tug-whatever?"

"Tascosa."

"I hope they've got a deep bed there."

"Why's that?"

"'Cause I'd love to get you in one for a couple of days, and then we could do it with each other until we couldn't walk."

He chuckled. "Sounds like my kind of a deal."

Her shoulders hunched to escape some of the stiffness in her back, she grinned. "Now, wouldn't that be fun."

"More fun than chasing Bridges, I'd say."

"Me too. How far from here do you think this place is that we're going to?"

"Three days' ride, maybe four."

She reached over and clapped his leg. "We may have to stop someplace before then—for a break, I mean." Then she wrinkled her nose and winked wickedly at him. "Well?"

"We will have to do that," he promised her.

"I guess Denny and Annie are getting it on somewhere."

He looked over at her. She'd noticed that about them too.

"And doing this and that. You saw them. They were anxious to get away from us to go after each other, weren't they?"

He laughed. "I really think they were. Denny is a good young man. He'll be a lot taller in life with her than he's ever been before."

"Where did he come from?"

He checked Buck, and she stopped too. "It's a long story he told me."

"Now you've got two of them to tell me."

He looked over the rolling hills carpeted in belly deep bluestem land that stretched from north to south in front of them. "We find some water and fuel, we'll stop early."

"Good. But we can always simply eat some jerky and then toss in the bedroll." She studied the high clouds moving up from the south. "It may turn real cool tonight. Feels like the sun's running out of power to me."

Slocum agreed. "Must be getting close to fall all right."

They crossed the next rise, and he reined up to look over a small outpost nestled alongside a tree-lined stream. This was west of the places that he knew well in the territory. The land was drier here than the part where the Chisholm Trail sliced across the territory.

"You figure they're down there—at that place in Texas you named?" She looked over at him.

"They aren't far ahead of us. They could be. I'm thinking we can make camp somewhere and wait till morning, check out the place then."

She nodded as if she was turning his idea over in her mind. "I'm ready to get off this horse. Mind you, I'm not complaining. Just ready to stretch my legs and detach my backside from this saddle."

"Not a bad idea." He booted his pony downhill.

They found a place where some boys had likely treated themselves to the water—for swimming, no doubt, for they'd worn the grass off the opening between the bigger trees hugging the bank. A fire ring marked the spot, and they'd probably caught some small bream and bullheads in the river to cook supper . . .

Slocum recalled those early days. Good times, joined by other boys his own age in Georgia, they'd swum naked until the sun about set on them, then they'd cooked fresh fish and dried by a big fire. They told lies about all the girls they'd fucked since the last time they were up there and how theirs had begged for mercy from their big dicks.

Hell, anyone looking around could see that none of them had more than six inches of manhood all shriveled up from the cold water. No one ever challenged a friend's bragging about it though—but they all knew they told concocted stories to make others think that in real life they were stallions. Actually, at that time in their lives they'd only ever watched, through a knothole in the barn, someone else getting himself a piece.

It wasn't long after that they found out that pussy was a better deal than jerking off in a circle. But the four or five neighborhood boys had a few summers of innocent wonderment, a gut-wrenching fear of getting caught at it, and they bravely talked about sex and what it would be like to really do it to a woman, black or white. They camped up there. Had a skillet, cornmeal and lard, and sometimes they burned the fish and made hush puppies so hard they could have been used as minié balls.

Slocum remembered when Tommy Jack Steele brought a girl up there the first time. She was their age or maybe a little older. After sundown, she'd be sitting on the ground in back of them, hugging her knees and rocking on her butt like she wanted something to happen.

Tommy Jack called her Shonie, and the others kept sneaking looks at her and raising their eyebrows in the fire's light when they turned back. No one moved, like they were all waiting for Tommy Jack to tell them what they could do.

Tommy Jack got up with his chest all puffed out and walked back and forth around the fire. The cicadas were really loud in the trees that summer.

Heddrow Smith couldn't stand it a minute longer. He point-blank asked what Tommy Jack Steele had brought her there for.

A snicker, then some nervous laughter went through the three others.

"Gawdamn you, Heddrow." Tommy Jack swore at him. "You reckon she's here to spout off her ABC's?"

Caught in a tight place, Heddrow shrugged and then wilted. "I didn't know. No one ever told me anything."

Then he looked around for some relief. But Slocum knew Tommy Jack wasn't letting up any on the boy. "Get out here, Shonie. This boy ain't never touched no real pussy. Come on, girl."

She shrugged and rose to obey him.

"Now, you get on your knees, girl," Tommy Jack set her

up facing them. "He ain't going to hurt you none."

She looked uncomfortable and folded her arms over her small breasts.

"Get out here, Heddrow."

"Why me?"

"Get out here and you get on your knees right beside her."

"Why me? I-I ain't done nothing."

"This is what I'm trying to get you to do." Tommy Jack sounded impatient as hell. "Now, here. You put your right hand under her skirt and reach under it. Then tell me what her pussy feels like. Sit still girl. He ain't a-going to hurt you none.

"You feeling it yet?"

Heddrow shook his head, looking awkward as he reached deeper.

Then under his breath, Tommy Jack told her to spread her legs apart more. "What you feeling for, Heddrow?"

Numb-like he nodded. "I found it."

"Good, good. Tell us what real pussy feels like."

"There's a crack and some stiff hair."

"Use your middle finger and push it in her. Can you do that?"

"It's tight—"

"Be still, girl," Tommy Jack said and squeezed her shoulder. "He ain't hurting you none."

They all half-laughed at his words, but things were too tight to let go and really laugh. Each one's ears hurt from all the bugs buzzing over them in the tree residences. Heddrow looked like he didn't know what was up her crotch, groping her under the short, ragged dress.

"Now, get your suspenders down and give her your dick," Tommy Jack said, taking his hand away from her.

Heddrow looked to the rest of the boys for some relief, but they all stared, hard faced, each fearing that Tommy Jack might make him be the next puppet. Then Heddrow raised up and dropped his suspenders, undid his fly and shoved down his pants so he was sitting on them.

"Jack him off, girl."

She made an angry face and then shuffled over to her victim. She took Heddrow's dick in her hand, and with her fierce pumping, in less than two minutes she had the white foam flying out the head of his hard-on.

Heddrow sprawled on his back and looked dead for a long moment. "God almighty, Tommy Jack, she done pulled my balls out the end of my peter."

"You'll get over it. Who's next?"

Slocum wasn't going to volunteer. Let Tommy Jack choose him. So he sat cross-legged in the noisy, insect-filled night and watched each one finger her while she jacked them off.

When it got to be his turn, he rose, shed his cutoff shorts and, with his erection in his fist, motioned for her to lie down on the ground. For the first time all night, she grinned big at the prospect of what he intended to do to her. Raising her knobby knees in the air, she spread them apart for his entry, knowing damn good and well what he aimed to do with her . . .

Horses unloaded and hobbled in the bloody light of sundown, Slocum saw that Meagen was busy building a fire. He had no idea what she'd fix, but he didn't care, watching her sweep the hair back from her face. Her cowboy hat rested on her shoulders as she worked.

"Boy, wouldn't some fresh beef go good right now?" She looked up and smiled at him

"If wishes were fishes—"

"Yeah, I know." Then she turned back to put several strips of bacon in the skillet over the fire. "There ain't nothing out here but coyotes and jackrabbits, is there?"

"At least it's a long ways from anything." He dropped to

his butt to sit and watch her cook. "It ain't populated at all. You getting tired of this business?"

"Naw. I ain't got a thing else to do. For that matter, I ain't sure what I will do with my life. Maybe go work in some brothel for excitement. Maybe there I could almost forget what's happened to my life. Those bastards killing my husband and taking me."

"That's not any answer. You could go run that ranch of yours. You have the feed put up. The hay fields cleaned up. Hire a few old cowboys, get some stock."

She nodded, still looking downcast. "It will be harder for me, being a woman."

"You're tough enough. You can handle it. Some nice guy will come down the road for you—if you want him."

"It won't be the same. . . ."

She took the hat off and set it on the grass, then leaned back with her hands behind her to brace herself. "After we eat this meager meal, let's get in the bedroll and you can make me forget—all this business."

He agreed, bobbing his head. "Where did you meet your husband at?"

"Carl came back from Kansas after two cattle drives and showed up at a dance. We lived west of Waco. My folks had a cow outfit, but my dad never had any boys—just four girls, and I was the oldest. So I was his hand. I never considered myself a girl. I even wore overalls to the dance. Carl came over and asked me to dance. . . .

"I shook my head and looked away like I always did when some boy came by for a dance. God, then he sat down on the empty bench—right beside me. Holding his hat in his hand like he didn't know what to do with it.

"I guess he asked me my name a dozen times, but I didn't answer, I was so embarrassed. I wanted to get up and run. Then my youngest sister, Mary Ann, told him that my name was Meagen. Oh, she was 'bout five then, and she started asking him questions. Like, what was he going to do to me? Oh, it got worse, so I jumped up and pulled him up to dance with me just to escape her. I stumbled around in my run-over boots and it never bothered him a bit. Like he was used to women who couldn't dance."

She got up on her knees and with a fork dished out the browned bacon onto one plate. Then using a rag for a hot holder, she took the skillet off the fire. "We can eat off one plate, can't we?"

"Sure," Slocum said and waited for her to continue.

"My, my." She shook her head and made a grim face. "You know, he was fifteen years older than me, or more. I never was certain. But he said he had money enough for us to start a ranch up there and he'd treat me nice if I'd put up with him."

"He wasn't hard to put up with, was he?"

"Not at all." She chewed on her lip. "I'll never regret a day in my life as his wife. I wished we'd had children, but I had a bad case of the mumps when I was twelve. A doctor told my mother back then I'd never have any kids." She shrugged. "I guess you take the cards dealt to you and go on."

Busy chewing on a piece of bacon, he nodded. "I'm amused at the thought of you being a tomboy."

She dropped her gaze. "I damn sure was one."

He chuckled, then his thoughts turned back to the present. Where were Bridges and his sidekick at? The last rays of sundown set the hills afire with their scarlet paint. They'd get him. He'd get both of them. They were marked men.

17

Barr awoke in his usual grumpy mood the next morning. Standing over him, bowlegged as a railroad tunnel he'd seen one time, was his man.

Kittles shook his head in disbelief. "Why, Mr. Barr, I swear if you don't look plumb rested."

"Well, I damn sure ain't rested. My back hurts, and I'm constipated." Why did he tell that drawling dumb sumbitch anything? Now Kittles would be telling him all kinds of remedies all day. No wonder Goodall had left that drawling bastard behind with Barr. "Mr. Kittles, go hook up the team."

"Don'cha think we should wait on Mr. Two Hawks?"

Barr scowled at the man. "That blanket-ass Injun ain't coming back."

Kittles swallowed hard. "Well, Miss Erma ain't got all your breakfast cooked yet, Mr. Barr."

"What's she been doing?" Barr pulled on his britches and tucked in his shirt.

"Doing? Why, she's been plumb busy fixing you a nice breakfast."

"Never mind." He stomped into his boots and went off to piss. He ought to do it on her fire. Damn, that girl and Kittles would drive him crazy. The dew shaken off his lily, he put it away, engrossed in wondering what in the hell Bridges was doing as he buttoned up his fly. They had the word he'd talked about going to Tascosa, Texas. If that worthless Two Hawks ever brought him those horses . . . Then Barr saw both of the worn-out horses lying down on the ground.

Horses never did that unless they were completely done. Damn, he'd have to wait for that Injun. He strode back to camp.

"Oh, Mr. Barr, looky, looky, he's a-coming. Sure enough he's a-coming. Yes sirree, he done be coming. Look at them ponies. They look fresh, don't they?"

They looked to Barr like some damn Injun pintos. Probably wouldn't go nowhere. It was too damn easy. There'd be something sour in the deal.

Kittles went and got the team up. On their feet, they shook like their hair was coming off. Maybe the Injun wouldn't notice.

Erma came over to Kittles, wringing her hands in the apron. "Breakfast is ready."

"I need to make this deal. Keep it warm." He left her. She'd heard him.

"Well, Mr. Two Hawks, how you been since I last seed ya?"

"Good."

"Which one goes on the right and which one goes on the left?"

Two Hawks blinked at him.

"One horse goes on this side." He held up his right hand, then he indicated the left.

Two Hawks shrugged. He didn't know.

"Mr. Hawks, have they ever been drove?"

He nodded. "Squaws take them for supplies."

"Well, that's good news, sir." Kittles grasped his hand and shook it, wrapped in both of his. "I'll just harness them, then. Which one is the riding horse?"

"Him." He meant the red and white one he had ridden in on.

"Good. I'll saddle him."

"Where is watch and money?"

"Mr. Barr, he's my boss. He has it all. He's right over there, sir." Kittles pointed him out like Two Hawks might not know him.

The Injun nodded, then went to Barr to get his money and watch.

Kittles put his blankets on the red piebald, then the saddle. Red snorted at him, but his action didn't bother the cowboy. He completed the job and hobbled him like nothing at all. Then he took the black and white one and fit the collar on him. The bronc acted spooked when Kittles tossed on the noisy harness. Like most men used to harnessing horses of all kinds and dispositions, he went on strapping the rigging on until completed, then he hobbled Black. The tricolor horse was a head slinger. Kittles waded into him.

Barr watched as the Injun rode off on Kittles's thin horse and led the team through the grass and mesquite brush. He soon was over the hill, and for Barr, that suited him fine.

The two horses harnessed and hitched, Kittles left the black hobbled so the team didn't wander off, then hitched up his pants and headed for Erma's cooking and smoky chip fire. She had fixed Barr a plate and coffee. He watched her serve Kittles.

No. He wasn't asking that dumb hillbilly a damn thing about them horses. Come from somewhere up there in Missouri. Shit fire, in the past few days he'd learned more about that man than he could remember about himself.

When breakfast was over, Erma hurriedly washed and Kittles dried the dishes. It took them forever to load the wagon.

"I don't want you or Erma hurt none. I'll jest drive them ponies around a little, if'n you'd hold my horse and when I get on the seat, pull them hobbles off the black one."

"Good. I can do that."

"I'd sure be mighty pleased for you doing that."

Kittles climbed on the seat and took the reins. Erma unhitched his horse from the buckboard. Barr slipped off the hobbles and backed away.

Reins in each hand, Kittles quietly clucked to them. Nothing. Barr closed his eyes. That damn Injun has screwed him—his man slapped them harder.

Then in an explosion, the pair reared and began walking on their hind feet. Then the team hit the ground racing. Kittles was standing up, fighting the bits, but the wagon raced out of sight with Kittles shouting, "Whoa! Whoa!"

Cowboy and horses topped the crest of the hill, flat-out going to the races. Sumbitch, he'd have a damn wreck and leave them stranded out there. No need to run after him, he'd never get far.

In disgust, Barr threw his hat on the ground and thought about stomping it to pieces.

"What will happen to Maynard?" Erma sounded concerned.

"Who gives a damn about him? I suppose that saddle horse you're holding will buck us off. I've got more bad luck than three men."

"Listen. Listen," she said. "Maynard's coming back."

Barr squatted on his heels, absently snapping off dry stalks of bunchgrass. "I bet he can't stop them. Wave at him when he goes by."

The open-mouthed team, ears back, came flying over the crest of the hill, and with his feet braced on the dashboard, Kittles sawed their mouths until they slid to a halt.

"They'll be just fine, Mr. Barr." He jumped down and still held the reins. "Here, you can drive them."

What was he getting into? Oh, damn. In a frenzy, Erma

quickly loaded the rest of her cooking things in the box in back, gathered her dress tail and then scrambled onto the seat.

"Why, Mr. Barr, they'll be just fine," Kittles assured him, still holding the reins as his boss climbed on the seat. Barr took the lines and shook his head.

Kittles ran for his horse. Keeping the reins tight, Barr turned the team in a wide, cautious circle. Both horses acted like they were walking on eggs. At last they slipped back onto the narrow road, and were stepping out—Barr still was not certain, guiding and holding them back so that they wouldn't run away.

A few miles down the road, Barr still wasn't convinced the Injun ponies might not break him in two. When two prairie chickens busted out for the sky from some low brush beside the road, the team spooked sideways. Erma suppressed a scream and her hand squeezed his leg. Barr stayed with them and held them from breaking and running away. It worked, but it sure upset his stomach.

What were Doss and his hired men doing? Had they caught up with Bridges? How would he ever know? Damn. He was trapped on this spring seat by these unbroken broncs that any minute might run off and kill him in a wreck.

And where was that damn Slocum? The headache began to pound in his temple.

18

The sun's golden crest breaking over the horizon, Slocum was deep in the bedroll on top of Meagen. With her silky legs wrapped around him, he savored her lithe body's moves and the obvious pleasure she shared with him. His eyes closed for him to savor the sensations every time he plunged in and out of her satin gates. Sneaking a peek from time to time he saw her open mouth tense in moaning as he hunched his skintight manhood into her.

Consumed in the wildfires of passion, their lovemaking grew more forceful. Her eagerness and needs urged him on. He shoved his aching erection to the bottom of her well, and it exploded in a screaming finality. When both found release at the same time, they collapsed in each other's arms.

"Should we get up?" she asked in his ear.

"Hell, I guess."

She braced herself up on her elbow and moved the hair out of her face. "We need to keep chasing Bridges."

"Oh, I agree." He closed his sore eyes and then tossed back the top cover. "Oh, here comes the reality of our lives."

She pulled him back and kissed him. "Thank you."

He smiled. "Pleasure was all mine, girl. All mine."

It was hard to leave a bed full of a woman like her. He got up, dressed and built a chip fire. The smell of the smoke from these types of fires never appealed to him, but it was the only fuel at hand. In a short while after they ate and with the low heat of the sun on their backs, they checked on the outpost. No word or sign that Bridges had been there. They had no grain for sale either. So Slocum and Meagen rode on, leaving the half-dressed white trader scratching his belly.

"Lots of nothing out here, isn't there?" she asked when they topped a ridge and looked over the deep draws in the grassland. All of this country had been Comanche land before the army shipped them off to the Oklahoma reservation. The buffalo gone, longhorns were taking their place.

"One more hill to cross," he said and laughed.

With the packhorse in tow, they traveled the narrow wagon ruts that wound off the high point into the deep canyon. Slocum hoped they'd find some water in the depth of this draw. It looked like a poor place for finding moon lakes, the water pools trapped in many places in this land. If the two of them didn't find some, it would be a long day for the horses without water.

A small seep was pooled in the bottom of the draw, enough water to refresh their horses. They stood by their mounts and let them slake their thirsts. Stiff from all the days in the saddle followed by sleeping on the ground, Slocum flexed his shoulders against the sore muscles.

"This has been half fun and half hell, hasn't it?" Meagen asked.

He laughed. "Oh, I've enjoyed it. You're a good traveler."

The horses finished drinking, and she checked her horse's girth. Slocum came up behind her and kissed her neck.

"Don't expect too much. This is a tough town we're going to."

"Is there no law there?"

"There's law, but it isn't very actively enforced."

Swinging into the saddle, she laughed and shook her head at his comments. "No active enforcement, huh?"

"You'll see."

That afternoon they passed through the crumbled adobe site where St. Vrain had built a trading post during the height of the buffalo hunting. All the wooden buildings had been torn down and removed from the site in this land where lumber was scarce.

"The buffalo hunters and traders held off hundreds of Cheyenne, Kiowa and Comanche warriors here. Some hunter with a Sharps .50-caliber shot an Indian a half mile away during the battle. Quanah Parker was wounded up here. Some bucks rode in and swept him up off the ground, saved his life. They were good at that."

"Not much here today." She stood in the stirrups and looked it over.

"No, just another place where men got killed settling this land. During the war, ten years before that attack, the mountain man Kit Carson brought a cannon and some four hundred men over here from New Mexico and fired it down the Canadian River at all the Indians camped along the river. Soon he decided that there were too many of them and went back home."

"Bloody ground," she said.

He agreed. Knowing where he was at also told him that in two days they'd be in Tascosa. Good. There were only two of the outlaws left. The toughest of the gang of killers and rapists to face them. Meagen pointed out a moon lake and they rode over there in the late afternoon.

He dropped heavily out of the saddle and unlaced the sweaty girth. A hot breath of pungent horse odor escaped from the wet saddle blankets when he hefted the rig off his horse's back. He set the blankets on the horn and spread them out to dry.

He sent Meagen off to find some fuel while he unloaded the other two horses. In a short while he had the packhorse emptied and Meagen's pony off grazing. While he was occupied, she piled up several mounds of dry cow patties. He soon ignited the fuel in a recent campfire ring he found and kindled up her cooking fire.

"Whew," she said and mopped her face on a kerchief. "We're getting better at this setting up, aren't we?"

With a hug, he caught and kissed her hard, then he winked at her. The sun would soon escape the panhandle, but they'd have a fire to cook upon. A tall cloud bank in the north concerned him. He watched the last rays of the sun dance on the high face of the clouds.

"We may have rain tonight," he said, setting up to cover their tack and panniers with a tarp—simply in case.

"I thought it never rained up here?"

"It don't often, but you can get a year's total in a couple of hours."

In the bedroll after supper, before he closed his eyes with his arms wrapped around her, the faint sound of thunder rolled across the high plains. Rain was coming.

Where were his enemies—Bridges and Horace, Barr and his men? Some were ahead, some behind them. He and Meagen in the middle—a tight place to be.

Half-asleep, she rolled over and kissed him. Her hand pressed his palm against her right breast. "You need me?"

"Maybe. . . ."

Small drops of rain began to splatter on their canvas cover. He kissed her again and tasted her tongue in the inky night. Deep in the cocoon warm with their body heat, they snuggled in passion's arms. He savored her silky body as they became connected and pushed as one for their pleasure. With him buried deep inside her, her contractions became stronger and she slipped into a dreamy world that must have rocked her brain. Moaning softly, she savored each thrust.

The rain let up, and he dared to view the world around them. More rain in the form of a tall dark cloud and strong lightning were coming out of the northwest at them.

"What do we do?"

"We better get dressed and get ready to move before the big one gets here."

"Fine." She sprang up and began dressing. In a few minutes he had the horses gathered and speedily saddled, and he undid the slickers tied on behind them. He slipped into his and then helped Meagen with hers. With panniers fastened on the crossbuck packsaddle, they whipped out the canvas and diamond hitch to cover their load. A stiff wind had begun to bring in the new rain. In the saddle, he led the way southwest under the stars. Tascosa was in that direction. He'd be glad to get this Bridges business over with. He looked back into the lightning-illuminated wall of rain encroaching on their vision—where were Barr and his men?

19

Barr was suspicious, watching the storm gathering, and also listening to the nice-nice chatter between Erma and that damn drawling idiot, Kittles, the next morning after breakfast.

"I got that team hooked up, Mr. Barr, fur you."

"I can see." He wanted to ask if they were still full of fire, but wouldn't dare. Kittles'd make a major speech out of that, and he'd have to listen to it all.

"Get your ass going, girl," Barr said under his breath as he went by her.

"I am, I am."

"You need some help, little lady?" Kittles asked, going to her defense.

Before he puked up his breakfast, Barr moved away from the two of them. He'd kill both of them if they planned to abandon him out here. How many more days was it to this Texas outpost? No communication. Exasperated, he paced around as the other two loaded the buckboard.

"Mr. Barr, she's all loaded."

He didn't dare speak and climbed on the seat. Kittles

handed him the reins and then took off his hat and nodded at Erma. "I think they'll be all right."

Sitting on the seat with the lines in his hands, Barr's stomach went sour. The stunted ponies acted ready to spring. He let out on the tension of the lines and the horses danced. Were they going to balk? To his relief they began to move the wagon from a standstill. A jerk on the tugs forced him to reposition his butt on the board seat as he braced his boots against the dashboard.

Erma sucked in her breath, but the team settled in and started moving at a trot.

Kittles said aloud, "Now, ain't they nice?"

Barr heard him all right and didn't answer. His attention was focused on the still-tense team as they climbed the steep grade. All he wanted was to get what was left of his money—Bridges could not have spent it all in the places he'd been at. But they needed to catch him, and soon. Were Doss and his crew doing it? He leaned back to slow down the horses.

Erma pulled on his sleeve. "Who are those men out there?"

Barr blinked at the four riders. They were out a good distance across the open grassland, but they were obviously interested in the three of them. Something he didn't like—two of them were bareheaded. They might be renegades, breeds or even some reservation jumpers. All he needed at this point was some freebooters looking for weak or easy targets to attack and rob.

Kittles brought his horse alongside Barr's side of the rig. "You seeing them riders out thar?"

Barr nodded. "Who the hell are they?"

"Damned if'n I know, but they look like trouble."

Barr agreed with a nod. But what could they get behind to fight them off? There wasn't a pimple to take cover behind. The team became his least worry.

"Keep your eyes on them and let me know if they move to intercept us," he said to Erma.

He heard Kittles, riding beside him, load his rifle. "Mr. Barr, I'll sure be with you when all hell breaks loose around here."

Hell breaks loose? Did he know that they were really some outlaw gang?

Barr nudged her with his elbow. "What are they doing?"

"Riding along as if sizing us up."

"Sizing us up?"

"Oh, they want to know who we are and whether they can run over us."

He shook his head. "They can't."

She shrugged like she wasn't as certain about that and hugged her elbows tighter to the sides of her body. Then, upset as she was, she started biting her short nails back to the quick. Glancing over at her made him sick to see her doing that.

How had he gotten into this mess? He had wanted to simply ranch. Honyockers were filing homesteads on his range. Most couldn't even speak English. This was American land, not meant for foreigners. They'd starve, plowing up the damn prairie to plant crops. He should be at home, sniping them off with his needle gun one by one.

It was a shame he didn't have that deadly accurate rifle with him. He could pick these bastards off with it like they were sitting ducks on a prairie pothole. His own Winchester was on the dashboard in a scabbard, but it wasn't anywhere near like his gun at the line shack.

Bastards! He slapped Erma's hand. "Quit biting your fingernails."

She obeyed and looked at him, shocked.

"I hate you doing that. You already have your fingers bleeding."

If somehow they lived through this day—he'd be damned surprised.

What were they waiting for? *Come on you sneaky devils. I want to kill you.*

20

Slocum and Meagen traveled hard for a day through the storm. Later the next day, Meagen used Slocum's field glasses to study the distant town. "It sure ain't much, is it?"

"Tascosa started out as a buffalo hunter's trading post when the big hunt was on up here, and it went downhill from there. Lots of rustlers and outlaws like Billy the Kid used it as a place to sell their stolen stock out of New Mexico. Horse trading was brisk and no one asked questions. Some twenty-four-hour poker games went on seven days a week. A man named Rojo brought two wagonloads of shady ladies up here from El Paso and he did a grand business. Gambling, wildcat whiskey and lots of prostitutes made this the party capital of West Texas. Mix men, whiskey and wild women, and you add lots of shootings to the list. I told you they don't enforce the law much out here. Businesses like a reckless boy's money. So it thrives. You caught sight of anyone you know?"

She dropped the glasses on the strap around her neck. "Not a one, but we're going in after dark, aren't we?"

He nodded. "Now is when I wish I had that boy. He

knows Doss and many other riders who work for Barr."

"I only know the ones who raped me."

"That's Bridges and Horace whoever."

"Them I'd know."

"We're going in after sundown, and you're going to cover yourself with a scarf and a blanket so they don't recognize you."

"Easy enough."

"It is just a dusty little town of adobe jacals, fighting chickens, cur dogs, bare-assed brown children and lots of wanted men hiding out."

"It will be dangerous?"

"Oh, yes, but all we have to worry about is Bridges and his henchman, as well as whoever is with Doss."

"You don't think Barr beat us down here?"

"I doubt it."

"Good."

After sunset, the two rode their horses to the edge of town and tied them to an old, broken-down wagon on the outskirts of the jacals. Some cur dog discovered their intrusion and began barking.

"What about him?" she asked about the dog's loud barking.

"These dogs bark so much, no one takes them serious."

"Good." She tossed the blanket over her head as a hood.

Slocum chucked a rock at the barker. The dog yelped like Slocum had hit him and ran off. They were rid of him anyway.

They walked past a row of adobe houses. Light streamed out the open front door of one along with wild Mexican music from the musicians inside. The very recognizable laughter of some *puta* sitting, no doubt, on a customer's lap rang out. Another bare-shouldered woman came to the door, drew a last mouthful off a marijuana cigarette and flipped the glowing pinched butt out in a high arc to land in the dust.

"Where is that big gringo?" she asked someone over her shoulder.

"Ah, Bridges. . . ."

A little ways farther, Slocum pulled Meagen off into the shadows. He whispered, "You hear her?"

"Yes, she said, 'Bridges.'"

"Sounds like we are damn close."

"Where is he at?" She searched around in the darkness.

"I expect him to come back here unless he found a better subject to entertain him."

"Was she pretty, the woman in the doorway? I only got a quick look at her."

"Wasn't a princess, but she'd do in a pinch."

She hit his arm lightly. "You men can tease about the damndest things."

"I only want to get this job over with."

"Look, Slocum. That's him—Bridges."

"You see Horace anywhere?"

She peered around in the starlight, then shook her head. "He's not with him."

"We better go find him, then."

Looking perplexed in the faint light, she asked, "What about Bridges?"

"I think that *puta* will keep him busy all night."

"I agree. But they usually aren't that far apart."

"Where is your amigo, my lover?" the woman asked when Bridges appeared beside her. She jumped up to kiss him and he caught her, holding her off her feet as they kissed.

"Oh, he'll be coming along," Bridges said to her between kisses. Then she made a loud shout, and he swept her up and carried her inside.

Outlaw number two was coming as well. Slocum and Meagen nodded at each other.

"Let's walk up this street and find a place to ambush him."

"Go." She turned him in the direction of the square and

clung to his left arm as they walked toward the center of town, in and out of the shadows, around a few scrubby trees. When he saw a man coming on the opposite side, he swung her around and kissed her. They were kissing hard when the man went by them. She gave a slight nod—it was him.

"Oh, señor, *por favor?*" Slocum said in his best Spanish.

"What do you need, grea-ser?" Horace began, but then stood shock faced, staring at Slocum's six-gun as Slocum jammed the muzzle in his big gut.

"I want your ass. One word, one shout and you're dead. Now be real quiet-like, turn around, and we're going back uptown. Make one wrong move, and the loose pigs will eat your carcass."

Meagen removed the Colt from his holster and nodded that she had it.

"I-I-I—"

"Shut up," Slocum ordered.

They walked with him back toward the center of town. Slocum recalled a merchant who had a hay storage shed on Royale Street. It was isolated enough, and no one would be in it until long after dawn. If they bound and gagged Horace good, he'd be there when they came back for him later.

Slocum jerked Horace up in his face so he could smell the whiskey breath on him. "Where's Bridges keep his money?"

"I don't know."

"You better get to recalling where it's at, or I'm pouring kerosene all over your privates and setting them on fire."

"You son of a bitch, you wouldn't do that to me."

"She would, if I don't."

"Oh, hell, I know who you are—you're Slocum. And that's the whore from—"

Slocum bashed him over the forehead with the barrel of his handgun and shoved him inside the barn's dark interior.

"Say one bad thing about this lady, I'm sticking this gun up your ass to the chamber and blowing your brains out the top of your head. You hear me?"

"I was only spoofing you about her. Damn, I'm bleeding."

Roughly, Slocum shoved the fat man down on his knees. "Now, where is this money you all stole from Barr?"

"I swear—"

"You're going to swear with your balls on fire. Meagen, look around in here. There's bound to be a can of coal oil and some good rope."

She lit a lantern and then blew out the match. "Now maybe I can find something. There's some good rope over here."

Slocum half dragged his prisoner by the collar over to where Meagen was and quickly bound him up. Horace screamed that Slocum was killing him when he set the knots on his wrists behind his back. To shut the man up, Slocum crammed his kerchief in the fat man's mouth. "I'll tell you when you can speak. You hear me?"

His prisoner nodded. The blood on his face looked worse than it actually was. Slocum had no use for this ruthless killer. He looped the rope's tail over the rafter and soon had a noose made around Horace's throat.

"When he's on his boot toes, tell me," he said to Meagen as he made Horace stand on the nail keg.

She bent over to look at the outlaw's feet and finally nodded at Slocum. Horace's neck was well stretched, and he was mumbling around the gag. Slocum ignored him, tying the neck rope off on a barn post across the aisle. He made certain the knots held tight on the neck rope.

"What's next?" She blew out the lamp and dropped the glass's lever. With the lamp hung on a nail, they went outside the stuffy barn.

"Bridges next?" she asked, having to half-run to keep up

with him until they reached the house where they'd seen Bridges. "You weren't really going to cook that part of him, were you?"

"He and Bridges don't deserve one ounce of your sympathy. They'll tell me where the money is or suffer the consequences. Men may think they're tough as nails, but by damn they won't be half as mean when they're smelling coal oil and feeling a cool liquid sliding off their bare bellies."

The piano man, playing some Southern music, joined with the sounds of some half-drunk whores, whose loud remarks escaped the jacal quarters.

Slocum, with Meagen behind him holding Horace's Colt .45, stood nearby where the doorway's light spilled out into the night. Six-gun in his fist, he charged through the entrance. The shocked women raised their hands in the air. Meagen made them be quiet and stand against the wall.

Satisfied that she had them under control, he went down the hall and listened.

When he heard that the woman in the room was talking to his man, Slocum used his boot to kick open the door. Then with his six-gun cocked and ready, he charged into the room. Slocum caught Bridges pulling up his pants, with the candle lamp showing that Bridges's erection was still swollen as he raised his hands high. His pants dropped to his ankles.

"Don't move an inch," Slocum said and shouldered the outlaw's holster and six-gun from off a ladder-back chair. "Horace is securely bound in a hay barn. So forget him. Put on your shirt."

"My pants . . ."

"You're fine. You won't need them where you're going."

The woman huddled on the bed, holding the sheet up to cover her nakedness. "What are you going to do to us?"

"You mind your own business," Slocum said to her, emptying Bridges's pants pockets. Then he discovered the money belt lying underneath the pants. Good. This must be Barr's money. He swung the canvas belt around his neck and then made the outlaw step down the hallway and into the lighted room.

Meagen looked shocked at the sight of his prisoner, then shook her head, holding the gun on the women. "You've got him."

Her eyes filled with anger and hatred. Slocum thought she was close to gunning him down right there.

"Don't sh-shoot me," Bridges begged.

"Slowly walk to the door," Slocum ordered. Meagen held the women back at gunpoint as Slocum and Bridges left the house of ill repute.

"You come running out screaming, you can expect to die." Then Meagen hurried after him to catch up. Looking back to check, she saw that no one came outside after them. "They're listening to me."

"Good."

When they reached the barn at last, Slocum tied Bridges's hands behind his back. Meagen lit the lamp and held it for Slocum to see by. Red faced and frightened standing on his toes on top of the keg, Horace gazed at them in shock. The gag muzzled his words. There would be justice dealt in this town for the pair of rapists and killers. Nebraska was hundreds of miles away, as was Kansas law for the killing of Meagen's husband and her rape.

Slocum made Bridges kneel on the floor while he made a noose. When he completed it, he put the rope around Bridges's neck and tossed the tail over the rafter.

"Who hired you to rape my friend's wife?"

"I ain't saying."

Slocum swung on the rope, jerking Bridges to his feet, and screamed at Bridges, "I said tell me!"

"Barr's man. Barr's man, Doss."

"Then you robbed Barr?"

"The sumbitch was holding out on me."

"Stand on this keg."

"No."

"You want your head caved in with my gun butt or are you going to stand on this keg?"

Bridges obeyed, and with the noose around neck, he stood on the keg, his hands tied behind him.

"You got anything to say for yourself?"

"I'll see you in hell!"

Slocum kicked away the small barrel. The rope creaked. Bridges made a gagging sound, then his feet paddled the air before he died.

Slocum never looked away. Next he went to where Horace was standing on his toes on the other barrel, breathing hard in and out of his nose with the scarf still stuffed in his mouth.

As the remaining outlaw teetered on the keg, Slocum stepped over to deliver the same justice to him. But Horace stepped off before Slocum could kick the barrel away. Horace's neck snapped and he went still, hanging there.

"Let's get to the horses. Barr and his bunch can't be far behind."

Woodenly, she nodded and looked back at the two swinging silhouettes from the doorway. "They won't rape anyone else now."

"No, they won't, but we've still got Barr and Doss to worry about."

Without another word, they hurried off under the stars. Mounted at last and leading the packhorse, they rode into town under a sky full of stars. Two more killers were gone. They needed to get some supplies and then head out. Slocum had no urge to talk to any lawman about the executions.

Only Barr and Doss remained. Slocum intended for them to return to Nebraska. The law could deal with them up there. Slocum himself was the bait. All he had to do was get them to follow him back up there.

21

Daylight strengthened, and Barr woke up. He'd been feigning sleep, listening to his two companions talking. Was Erma planning to run off with Kittles? He'd wondered for the past few days about her loyalty to him. That damn drawling hick was surely trying to steal her away from him. If Barr wasn't so weak, he'd shoot the bastard and leave him for the buzzards. But he depended too much on the both of them.

And also, he wasn't sure they were even close to Tascosa. There was nothing out here but more dry rivers, jackrabbits, scorpions and rattlers. He was dead broke—maybe he could wire his banker in North Platte and get the man to wire some money to him.

"Any sign of those four?" he asked Kittles.

"No sirree. I ain't seed them, but we're close to that town."

Erma brought him some coffee and a tin plate of food. Then she apologized, "That's all we have to eat."

He looked hard at the fistful of fried potatoes. Then he nodded that he understood.

"I guess we're going to have to shoot us some jackrabbits today," Kittles said, squatting in his knee-high boots. "I ain't seen no deer or even an antelope in days, and then they was too far off to shoot."

Barr nodded. What had the two of them eaten for breakfast? Ate all the good stuff, probably, and left him the potatoes.

"I see one today I'll damn sure be ready to shoot him. Yes sirree. I'll drop him in his tracks. By wilikers, it's getting tough out here."

"No sign of Doss either."

"I don't know where that feller went to. I'm positive we ain't on his tracks anymore. He just went poof, like smoke. No sirree, he ain't close to us."

Where was his foreman at? Had he caught up with Slocum by this time? Maybe he'd even found Bridges and got his money back. The fried potatoes and gyp water coffee made his guts roil.

At last they were on the road. Erma was getting slower and slower about breaking camp. He ought to leave her ass out here somewhere—but she drove. He felt too weak to even sit up and at last made her stop and he got in the back and tried to sleep, but the buckboard ride was too rough.

Then the report of a rifle shattered his attempt to sleep. He bolted upright. "What is it?"

"I think Maynard shot an antelope." Erma reined in the team.

Barr sat up and blinked at the sight of Kittles far out on the prairie getting off his horse and reaching for his belt knife. Might be a good thing that Barr hadn't shot him after all. They could stop and cook some of the meat.

Erma drove the buckboard slowly out toward the hunter and his kill. When they arrived, Kittles had the antelope's belly split open and was hacking off some raw liver. He shoveled strips in his mouth with both of his hands.

She quickly joined him on her knees and started in on the feast.

"Good as we need," Kittles mumbled with his mouth full of liver.

"Yes." She gasped, with her face full like a pocket gopher.

"Stop! Stop!" Barr screamed at both of them.

She froze with her mouth full. Fresh blood ran off her chin. "You don't know. You were sleeping." She took a deeper breath. "You were the only one who's been eating for the last two days."

He collapsed on his butt. They'd been protecting him for two days. Doing without anything to eat. He threatened to vomit up his entire guts; then he choked up bile from his own sour stomach. It gagged him hard. Then he passed out.

When he awoke he smelled the chip fire and heard the meat sizzling. His stomach was so sour he wasn't sure he could even eat a well-done piece. The stench of the sour guts and butchering made him look over the side of the wagon for another place to throw up.

"Listen, listen," Kittles was repeating to him. "You've sure got to eat or you're going to die. She gave you all the food we had 'cause we knowed you was the weakest of us three."

Bleary-eyed, Barr nodded. "You have any idea where that gawdamn town is at?"

"Not rightly. But I'll sure find it. I ain't never been in this country before. I made two trips from South Texas to Kansas before with herds, but this ain't on that road. Why, we're way west of it."

"How're you going to find it?"

"Soon as I find something, I'll let you know."

Downcast and shaking his head in disbelief over this entire episode, Barr slid off the tailgate of the buckboard. Leaning on his elbows for support, he sighed. "These are some of the worst days of my life. I can't think for the headaches I have. My stomach must have an ulcer big as my hat. And I'm out here with you two."

"You wanting us to leave? Right now?" Kittles acted affronted.

"No. . . no. But I don't know what to do—how to handle all this. . . ."

"Well, you jest sit back. Me and Erma're going to take care of you."

"I need a doctor. I need—oh, shit, I need so many things."

She brought over a pan of browned meat and set it in front to them on the wagon floor.

"Better eat this. I'll cook you some more."

"Mighty nice of you, missy," Barr said. "Mighty nice."

Back half-asleep, Barr heard her say, "He never ate much. . . ."

22

Early the next morning, Slocum had already dickered for his supplies and an extra packhorse. He and Meagen were loading it all in front of Supinosa's General Mercantile when suddenly he told her to duck, and she obeyed. A whiskered rider on a paint horse alongside a buckboard being pulled by a calico team and driven by a young woman went by them.

"What's happening?" she asked in a whisper.

"They've stopped at the sign that says 'Doc's Office.' They have a passenger in the buckboard. Must have gotten hurt."

"Who is it?"

"I'm guessing, but I'd say it was Barr."

A man who Slocum imagined was some kind of doctor started down the stairs, and the bearded ranch hand with the peaked hat shouted to the physician. "Hurry, Doc. Mr. Barr is close to dying."

"Hold your horses. I can't fly. What's wrong with him?"

Slocum couldn't hear their conversation as he watched the doctor use his stethoscope to check Barr's heart.

"What are they doing?" she hissed.

"Just checking him. He must have beat Doss getting out here. Let's lead these ponies up the street and then around the corner before we mount up."

In a few minutes they were headed north, but Slocum was scoping the country for any sign of Barr's gun hands coming.

"What do you think happened to the rest of them?" she asked.

He smiled at her and shook his head. "I have no earthly idea. But I don't want to be around here when they start asking questions about the hangings."

She laughed, and the meadowlarks called to them as they short-loped away from the town in the waving grass. They'd have frost before they got back to Meagen's place in Kansas.

During the next few days, the question ran through Slocum's head: did she plan to stay on her ranch? He wasn't planning to press her for an answer. She'd come a long ways since Bridges's gang had left her naked and sore in the soddy, with her dead husband blocking the doorway.

"You want to check on your place when we ride through there in a few days?" he asked her late in the afternoon.

Chewing on her lip, she shrugged. "Do I have to tell you today?"

"No, but you need to decide soon."

They reined their horses down to a walk. "We'll be in Dodge tomorrow night," he said to her.

"So soon. I will have to decide, won't I?"

He gave her a sharp nod.

"I know I can't have you, but will you come by and see me sometimes?"

"You can't tell where or when I'll show up."

"That makes it hard. I could simply ride where you go."

"But you need to eat and have a roof over your head. Women are made like that."

She agreed. "But it has been a nice honeymoon for the most part with you. The one that Carl and I had never took." Her chin bobbed. "So I'll have good memories anyway."

"Don't make it sound so much like punishment."

"Damnit, Slocum, I don't have to like you leaving me. All right, we'll get my team and some supplies in Dodge."

He nodded that he'd heard her.

Things went smoothly. At her sister Karen's place outside of Dodge, Karen's husband, Arthur, hired Meagen a dependable ranch hand named Lyle. He was to join her on the place in two days, driving up her team of Belgian draft horses and bringing the supplies she needed out to the ranch.

Her plan was to have Slocum by himself for the next two days, then she'd return to her role of ranch owner. Wrapped in their slickers, they made it through driving rain to her place. The wind driving the storm came out of the northwest and made them put their shoulder to it. Despite her protests, after they unloaded the packhorses, he sent her to the house to build a fire while he put the horses up.

The house's interior had begun warming from the pot-bellied coal stove when he came inside out of the hard-driving rain and stood on the rag rug while he took off his slicker. The rubber coat and his soaked hat were hung on wall pegs.

"Winter just blew in," she said and laughed. "Coffee is about ready. I'm making eggs, fried potatoes and biscuits. That be enough?"

He came over and bear-hugged her. "I'd eat bread crumbs to be with you."

"That would get quick."

"Wish we had time to try it."

"Oh, Slocum." She cupped his face in her palms and looked him square in the eye. "There's lots and lots I'd like to do to you."

He pushed her away to go work on the food.

"Where are you going next?" she called out.

"Despite all Barr's losses he will go back to North Platte. It's where his ranch and livestock are at. So in time, if he doesn't die, he has to come back. I'm going to meet him and his henchmen up there and even the score for Charley and Minnie."

"What about the boy with the older woman?"

"I'll stop by and speak to Denny and Mrs. Looper."

She winked knowingly. "They may not need company."

"Surely they can take a little time off." They both laughed.

The second morning, after waking up before dawn to the sound of ice pecking on her roof, Slocum and Meagen had a pleasure-filled session under the covers. She didn't want to let go of him, but in the end, she hurriedly dressed and made him breakfast. After that they languished in each other's arms for a long time before he left for the Looper place with one packhorse trailing him. In the wet wintry blast, he wondered if he could find her outfit. When he located the spring-fed creek, he rode up to the head of it. He found a small new sod house with a temporary canvas roof tied on it. The wind was slapping it around, and when he shouted at the front door, Denny came to answer it in his britches and long underwear top.

"Slocum." He waved and called, over the roar of the nature's forces, for him to come in. His horses hitched at the new rack, Slocum ran inside the structure with Denny.

"How did it go?"

"Bridges and Horace ain't with us anymore."

"Good." Denny took his hat and slicker and hung them up.

Mrs. Looper came out from behind a Chinese folding screen, adjusting the hem of her blouse. "Good day, Slocum. We—we weren't thinking about anyone finding us, I'm afraid. But we're very pleased that you came by."

The blush on her face amused him when he said, "I'm

going back to North Platte, so I won't be staying long."

"What about Barr?" Denny asked.

"He has too much up there not to come back for it. I'll be waiting for him. I want him hung in North Platte, so folks can see what happens to SOBs like him."

"You know, his hired killers shot my best friend when they raided her place."

"Yes, I know."

"Are you going to need help arresting him?"

Slocum smiled at the cloth ceiling popping overhead on the fresh cut rafters. "You have enough work here."

Mrs. Looper and Denny both laughed. "Guess you're right."

The next morning, Slocum prepared to leave under a clearing, cold sky after shaking hands with both of them. Mrs. Looper announced, before he left, that they planned for Slocum to attend their wedding the following June first. He agreed to be there and rode off with his breath making large clouds of vapor.

Staying overnight with farmers and others along the way in the more populous farm country, he swung north toward North Platte. He arrived in the river city two days after Thanksgiving.

He picked up Sheriff Garner at his office. They went for lunch and found the cook still serving leftover turkey meat in the restaurant. Over their plate lunches of turkey, mashed potatoes, dressing and cooked carrots, Slocum told him that Bridges and Horace were no longer in circulation. That satisfied the lawman, and he didn't dig any more. Then he told Garner that the other two outlaws in the gang were not going to be counted on the next census either.

Garner looked over at him. "What about Udall Barr?"

"He was real sick when they took him to the doctor down in Tascosa, but if he lives he'll come home. I'll be waiting for him."

The lawman nodded. "Guess you're right about that."

"When he comes home, I'm going to face him down. He hired Bridges and brought all this on."

Garner nodded. "Folks owe you another thank-you. I don't know another man who could have tracked down those killers. You need my help, let me know."

"I'll count on it."

They parted after the meal.

Next he took a bath in the Chinese bathhouse. After a shave and haircut with the sweet-smelling tonic filling his nose, he secured Buck and the packhorse from the livery and rode out to see about Leta Couzki.

Snow was melting and the ride was a slushy one. The bright reflection off the melting white stuff made his vision hurt riding out there. When he came up the swale, splashing through several inches of water rushing downhill, Leta came out of the tent and used her hand to shade her eyes.

"That you, big man?"

"It ain't St. Nick." He laughed.

"Boy, are you a great-looking break from my boredom up here. I've been going crazy."

He stepped down and she gathered her dress to rush to him. In a great sweep he took her up in his arms and went sideways, ducking under the peak of the tent door. She kissed him hotter than fire with her tongue like a branding iron before he eased her down.

Whew! He swallowed hard, looking at her from head to toe. What lay ahead had him trembling with excitement. They looked at each other with knowing grins and then began stripping off clothes as fast as they could. In seconds their cool skin was in contact, and they were piled in the bed under a mountain of covers.

He felt well situated on top of her. With his rising tool nested between her legs, the two of them moved their hips to find entry. Impatient, at last she stuffed him inside her and then let out a cry. Her arms wrapped around him, she hunched her butt toward him and buried his throbbing dick deep into her hot cunt. From there on it was a free-for-all, with each of them searching for their own relief, striving to reach that peak and fly away.

When he at last exploded inside her and sagged down on top of her in relief, they twisted to lie side by side. His hand kneaded her top breast and she pushed it at him—smiling. "Nice homecoming, hombre. You got ten more like it?"

"Maybe a dozen."

She laughed aloud at him. "Even you don't have that many in you, stud horse. I heard you went to Texas. Did you?"

"Yes, great country."

"Well, my house is going up much slower than I thought, and I'm afraid I'll be in this drafty tent all winter."

"Can't you find a cabin or house to live in? This tent is going to be real cold this winter."

"So far, not much luck."

"It's why I like San Antonio for Christmas."

She laughed. "You were just down there."

"I was as far away from San Antonio at Tascosa as it is from Nebraska." Then he squeezed her breast and she reached over to kiss him.

Her hand went deep and found him. "Let's try this again. I'm sort of liking it—your way."

He shook his head, scrambling on top again. "You like it any way."

"Well." She raised her eyebrows. "I guess I do."

They spent the day talking, napping, fucking, sleeping and having sex again. Eventually, he got up and dressed to go see about his horse. With Buck unsaddled and both of their horses fed hay in her small corral, he looked over the gray, cloudy sky. More winter weather coming.

23

"Bridges is dead?"

"Yes, sir, Mr. Barr, sure enough, they found both of them hung in a hay shed this morning." Kittles was beating his leg with his hat.

"Who did it?"

"Well, a man accompanied by a woman took Bridges out of a house—no one knew him—a big man, and she wore men's clothing and packed a .45."

"Do you think it was Slocum?" Barr stood on the porch of the hotel in the early morning light and shook his head.

"Well, I kinda thought about him."

"Who's got my money?"

Kittles shrugged. "No one mentioned it, Mr. Barr. Nobody."

"He couldn't have spent it all. He had enough money to last him for a year in this backcountry."

"Mr. Barr, I don't know where your money is at."

"What funeral home has Bridges's body?"

"I don't know."

"Find out. I want to know if he still has it on him or who stole it."

Kittles frowned. "You reckon we should talk to the law here first?"

"Screw the law. You go examine him and ask questions."

"But—but they might object."

"Object! You work for me. Those two bastards robbed my safe! They beat me senseless for no reason. You go and find out where that money is at."

"I'll do that."

"And be quick. If we don't find it today, they'll cover it up and we won't be able to trace it."

"Yes sirree, I'll do that, Mr. Barr."

Barr watched the bowlegged hick in his knee-high boots stalk down the street. Kittles'd be no help. Why, that drawling idiot had given up finding his money before he even left him.

Where in the hell was his money at anyway? He hadn't seen hide nor hair of Doss and his men since they got into Tascosa twelve hours earlier. He had more incompetent people working for him. All of them were too dumb to find their own asses with both hands. If he ever overcame this dizzy business, he'd run them all off and start over.

His head whirled and he caught a porch post to save himself from falling. Tascosa leaned on a forty-five-degree angle and his vision swarmed. In seconds his sight went black, and he slumped to the porch.

Erma's voice directing some men packing him upstairs was the next thing he heard. ". . . there. Put him on the bed easy."

"You need anything else, ma'am, you just call."

"He'll be all right in a little bit. Thanks," she said, ushering them out the door.

She turned to Barr. "You know you aren't well enough to go off by yourself like that. Why do you keep doing it?"

"I was fine." His weak voice sounded rusty to him.

"You weren't fine. You need to be under a doctor's care. While you were out, I got a telegram from your banker. They're wiring us five hundred dollars to pay our expenses back to Nebraska."

"Good," he said and closed his eyes. The inside of his forehead was trying to crash out of his skull. "Get me some medicine. I can't stand this pain any longer."

"You know if anything happens to you, as your mistress I will have nothing. If you die, who will get your ranch besides that banker?"

"What the hell—? Get the medicine."

"You are not listening to me. I want you to marry me."

He raised up on his elbows and blinked at her in disbelief. "Do you want your damn ass beat?"

"Tell me, tough guy. How will you get back to Nebraska?" She stood back, out of his reach, holding the medicine and spoon.

"No one threatens me—"

"What you are saying is no one threatens you when you're well. You aren't well, Udall Barr."

"Why, you little bitch. After all I've done for you—"

"You haven't done anything for me but rob me of my virginity without any respect and rut on me like a boar hog." She threatened him with the spoon.

"Give me the medicine," he pleaded and then slumped back on the bed. The outburst had drained his strength.

She poured the precious medicine in the spoon. "I want to get married to you today."

In defeat, he nodded and exhaled in surrender. "All right— I'll marry you."

He never knew how much later, but he mumbled through the man's words required of him, barely able to hold her hand. Erma stood beside him as he lay on the bed and prompted him.

". . . now pronounce you man and wife."

She kissed him on the forehead and went to the door with the man who had performed the ceremony.

"Sure hope you get stronger, Mr. Barr," the man said and left the room.

"Think you're smart . . ." She smiled for the first time he remembered and gave him another large spoonful of laudanum.

"You rest now, darling."

Darling? She'd never called him that before.

In a peaceful state of suspension resulting from the medicine, Barr heard her chewing the asses off Doss and the others.

"Where did Slocum go?" Erma sounded mad as hell. "What did he do with the money? Kittles found no sign of it at the funeral home—Slocum has to have it. How did he beat them all to Bridges and then get out unseen except by a couple of whores? And where in the hell have you been?"

Doss complained that they'd never been out this way before and had taken the wrong fork in the road. They only got themselves finally turned the right way around when they ran into Goodall, who did know the area and decided to stick with them since they were all after the same people. But then they'd had a horse go lame, further slowing the group since there'd been some shifty-looking characters shadowing them for a couple of days, and they didn't dare split up in case the outlaws got up the gumption to attack. When she didn't let up on them, Barr smiled to himself. She was going to make a tough boss. He fell back into a deep sleep.

Later she fed him a bowl of soup and then gave him another big spoonful of medicine. She told him to rest.

He could have sworn that sometime in the night she was buck naked in the bed next to him and Kittles was on top of her screwing her ass off. She had her ankles wrapped around his neck, folded up like a jackknife, and Kittles was prodding her ass with a huge donkey dick.

"Oh, oh, Erma, you're so wonderful," that hick called out, giving her all of his yard-long erection.

His wife—that hillbilly—in his own . . .

Two days later, during the small time when he was aware of anything and not deeply sedated as he was the rest of the day, he decided that she was packing to leave.

Her answer to his smallest question was for him to rest and take more medicine, which she'd then force on him. Early the next morning he could see the stars in the sky when they carried him down to his pallet in the buckboard. Minutes later they headed out of town. Someone also accompanied them with a farm wagon loaded with bedrolls and supplies for the trip back to Nebraska. She had it all organized.

Barr lost track of the days. Vaguely, he could recall Erma waking him and administering medicine to him. Then he watched her and that high-crowned hat Kittles drive off in the rig for Dodge City. Barr wanted to tell Doss what his wife and that damn Kittles were doing to him, but he fell asleep.

He guessed his money, which the bank had sent him, was what bought the fancy blue dress with all the ruffles on it that Erma wore when he saw her next—though when exactly that was, he didn't know.

"Darling," she said, cheery-like, fussing over him in his bedroll. "Do you feel any better this morning? Oh, you poor dear, you must need more medicine." Then she leaned closer and whispered in his ear, "Are you ready to have our honeymoon tonight?"

Barr blinked at her. What did she mean? Hell, he couldn't even get a hard-on.

24

Slocum was snuggled under the covers, with Leta's body heat making the bed a heated cocoon. He had planned to ride over to the Farley ranch—all he needed was the ambition to leave his warm world.

"Oh, hell," she finally swore in surrender. "I'll make us some breakfast so you can go."

She rose and pulled an undergarment on over her head. He watched her wiggle it over her well proportioned body. A little saggier than he could recall the original one being, but still one made to lay up with and dispense to. Some women were good but harder to fit with—she fit like a spoon. Tight enough but not too—he shook his head. His brain had begun swirling with sex. Damn, he loved it—each woman a little different and each one loveable.

After he ate the meal she prepared, he dragged his saddle out and tossed it on his horse. He also fed her horse and, with her wrapped against the north wind in a blanket observing him, he loaded up the packhorse he'd borrowed from Minnie and completed getting ready. Finally, he hugged and kissed her good-bye.

"Be careful," she said, "and come back soon."

"I may be gone two or three days by the time I ride up there."

"I understand. I need to go into North Platte and check on my carpenters. If I'm not back when you get here, wait for me."

They parted with a hard separation and he short-loped his fresh pony. Dark had settled before he reached the Farley ranch. Minnie met him at the door and blinked.

"Slocum, what are you doing back? Where's Denny?"

"Well, Denny is running a ranch down in Kansas for another lady. How are you?"

He hugged her and she invited him inside. The warm, snug house wrapped its warmth around him, and he realized anew why a tent wasn't the answer to winter north of the Platte River.

"Have you eaten?"

"No."

"Good, I have plenty of food. I'll make you something. Tell me all about Texas."

"Bridges, Horace and the other two aren't with us anymore."

She looked at the ceiling and shook her head. "God bless them."

"Barr, I guess, has not recovered from the beating Bridges gave him that night when he robbed Barr."

"Bridges robbed him?"

"After he left here that night, I'm pretty certain he robbed and beat up Barr."

"Oh," she said, slicing white potatoes into the hot grease.

"Barr's the one who hired him to come up here."

"That yellow dog. I'm sorry you had to make that long trip for me."

"There isn't anything to be sorry over. I have something for you."

She blinked. "What is it?"

"The money Bridges stole from Barr."

"Oh, Slocum you don't owe me any money."

"Yes, I do—or rather, those bastards owe it to you."

He rose, turned his back and drew the canvas belt out from under his shirt. Then he turned and put the belt on the kitchen table. "He owes this to you."

"I can't take it. It seems like blood money to me. It would remind me of that horrible night all over again."

"Minnie, it's your money. Barr and Bridges and the others owe you that."

She broke out crying, and he held her in his arms.

"Why me?" She swept plenty of tears from her eyes and on his shirt. "Why me?"

"I can't bring Charley back. I can't restore that night the four of them attacked you. Minnie, you're the one who gets it."

"Oh, Slocum, it seems so wrong. Me taking it."

He held and hugged her, then at last she let him eat his supper and they talked some more.

"What will you do about Barr?" she finally asked.

"I'll come to that fork in the road one day and decide then what I'll need to do."

"You rode clear back here to give me this money?"

"No, ma'am. I came back to settle with him here, where he was running over people like you. I wanted this to be a lesson to all these land grabbers like him."

"Will he make it back?"

"I don't know, Minnie. Only time will tell."

"You can stay here as long as you want."

"I have a place to stay. Thanks. Thanks very much."

"Charley told me you were like this." She nodded that she understood.

In the morning, he'd head back to Leta Couzki's—but first he had one more thing to check out. It wouldn't be far out of the way.

25

Barr wasn't sure where they were at. Kansas or Nebraska maybe. Erma held him to stand up to urinate. His body was too weak for him to even try to stand alone. The hands would load him in the back of the buckboard for her. His shoulders shook when he coughed hard. Somewhere he had caught a bad cold. It sounded deep, but he didn't worry about a thing; he felt free in the trance the medicine brought on him.

"When will we be home?" he asked, bleary-eyed, taking the second spoon of laudanum she poured for him.

"They say soon. Here, take the rest of your medicine."

"Good . . . good. I want to be home with you—"

"You don't start getting better soon, I'll have to give you three spoons at a time."

He waved her away in a dreamy voice. "I-I'll be fine. Fine as . . ."

His days became even further away from reality. She spoon-fed him, but he ate less and less. His wife kept up her good spirits, feeding him at mealtime and giving him his medication. Devoted and kind, they soon were back at the home ranch, and Mozelle came out to see Barr's wasted form when they carried him in.

Through his dim vision, he watched Erma proudly show her the wedding license. Then he saw the older woman turn her rage at his wife. He couldn't hear Mozelle's words, but he knew she was mad. Then she stomped out of the room and soon returned with a valise, wearing her driving clothes to leave.

Erma told one of the hands to take her to town. Then Erma smiled at Kittles, who stood there beside her. Quickly she whispered something in his ear and he clapped both knees. Barr read that hick's lips: "*By golly, we're rid of her too.*"

The funeral for Udall Barr was less than a week later. Folks noticed that only Barr's wife, Erma, and one of his hired men were there for the services. Oh, the banker was there all right, but the rest of the regular funeral attendees skipped the program.

A few questions were asked around town about his foreman, Doss, and the others.

"Got 'em all better jobs, yes sirree," her man Kittles told them. "Every one of them, when we got back, went off and got themselves a lot better paying job. Where? Oh, why, jest all over."

Slocum stayed out at Leta Couzki's, and he'd made some trips here and yonder. Finally he rode into town and met with Sheriff Garner. It was a nice day, with the temperature above freezing and the sunshine slanted in the office windows from the south.

"We need to take a ride," Slocum said.

"What did I do wrong now?" Garner asked, looking up from a wanted poster.

"I want to solve some crimes for you."

"You have some good evidence?"

"I sure do."

Garner stood up and put his wool overcoat on and then his felt hat. "I'm damn sure ready for that treat."

They collected Slocum's horse at the rack out front and walked the hard frozen ruts up to Pierce and Sons Livery. Garner wore his thin leather riding gloves and kept using the webs of his fingers to drive them on. "I'm curious. Which crime did you solve?"

"Oh, I want you to see my evidence and you decide. It may answer a million questions."

"What led you to this evidence?" Garner asked.

"You did, once upon a time, and we found nothing."

"What's materialized here?"

"Evidence."

After an hour's ride, they drew up at Barr's line shack.

"Well, I recall this place. What did you find?"

"Took me a few trips up here to ever locate it. Come on inside."

They hitched their horses and went inside the wagon board front door. Slocum crossed the floor and lifted up a well-fitted trapdoor. Both men knelt at the hole, and Slocum drew out the canvas bag.

With care, they unwrapped the long rifle, and Garner whistled at the sight of it.

"Who in the hell do you think this weapon belongs to?" the sheriff asked, looking over the well-oiled and well-kept gun.

"Want to guess?"

"Barr?"

Slocum nodded.

Garner looked at him hard. "How can I prove it?"

"That's his signature for the ammo on that receipt in the bag."

"Whatever possessed him to kill all those people?" Garner asked, rising up from the floor.

"I'd say the man hated people. Like he hated my friend Charley and didn't want him in this world any longer."

"I'm grateful to you," Garner said and shook his hand. "If you ever need a favor, call on me."

The next morning, Slocum gave Leta a long good-bye kiss, saddled his pony and rode south again. He might make San Antonio before the Christmas holiday. His and his pony's breaths made large steam clouds. A flake or two of snow flitted in the wind. San Antonio and the dark-skinned young women dancing in the warm sunshine beckoned him.

He waved his hat a last time at Leta.

Watch for

SLOCUM AND THE TERRORS
OF WHITE PINE COUNTY

384th novel in the exciting SLOCUM series
from Jove

Coming in February!